"You've Got That Rough-And-Ready Look," Taylor Said.

"Rough-and-ready, huh? I guess if that's what you need..." Mack shrugged, trying to be helpful. "I could tie a bandanna around my head and wear an ammunition belt strung across my chest."

Taylor smiled. "That would be a lovely touch. Not too stylish, though."

He raised one eyebrow and held her gaze. "I've never been known for my style."

Taylor felt like a woman in a trance, mesmerized by his dark eyes, soothed by his low voice. "No? Just what are you known for?"

"Action," he answered softly, his head tilting back. "Performance. Coming through in the clutch."

Dear Reader,

You can tell from the presence of some *very* handsome hunks on the covers that something special is going on for Valentine's Day here at Silhouette Desire! That "something" is a group of guys we call "Bachelor Boys"... you know, those men who think they'll never get "caught" by a woman—until they do! They're our very special Valentine's Day gift to you.

The lineup is pretty spectacular: a *Man of the Month* by Ann Major, and five other fabulous books by Raye Morgan, Peggy Moreland, Karen Leabo, Audra Adams and a *brand-new* to Silhouette author, Susan Carroll. You won't be able to pick up just one! So, you'll have to buy all six of these delectable, sexy stories.

Next month, we have even more fun in store: a *Man of the Month* from the sizzling pen of Jackie Merritt, a delicious story by Joan Johnston, and four more wonderful Desire love stories.

So read... and enjoy... as these single guys end up *happily* tamed by the women of their dreams.

Until next month,

Lucia Macro
Senior Editor

Please address questions and book requests to:
Reader Service
U.S.: P.O. Box 1325, Buffalo, NY 14269
Canadian: P.O. Box 1050, Niagara Falls, Ont. L2E 7G7

RAYE
MORGAN
YESTERDAY'S OUTLAW

SILHOUETTE *Desire*®

™ Published by Silhouette Books

America's Publisher of Contemporary Romance

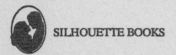 SILHOUETTE BOOKS

ISBN 0-373-05836-5

YESTERDAY'S OUTLAW

RAYE MORGAN

favors settings in the West, which is where she has spent most of her life. She admits to a penchant for Western heroes, believing that whether he's a rugged outdoorsman or a smooth city sophisticate, he tends to have a streak of wildness that the romantic heroine can't resist taming. She's been married to one of those Western men for twenty years and is busy raising four more in her Southern California home.

In memory of Nick Howe, my son's best friend, who laughed at romance but was my French phrase expert anyway.

One

Wanted: Hired gun for small Hawaiian ranch. Position temporary. Salary negotiable. Contact T. Taggert, Kohala District, the Big Island.

Mack stared at the ad for a moment. If it weren't for that classified, ripped from a Los Angeles newspaper, he wouldn't have come home. And right now he was thinking it was a shame he'd seen it at all.

Sighing, he stuffed the ad into the pocket of his jeans and turned slowly, looking at the changes the small air terminal had gone through since he'd learned to fly at this field almost twenty years ago.

Memories. Who needed them?

Not the men who ran this field, evidently. Joe Corman had logged him in right after he'd landed and rented out space to him for the ancient crate he'd flown in on without once recognizing him or his name. They'd never been friends. In fact, Joe used to curse at him and try to chase him away more often than not. But still, you'd think he would remember.

"Hey, you got any rental cars?" he asked the old-timer working behind the counter.

The man looked up, his shaggy gray hair framing eyes as blue as antique china, and shook his head. "Naw. We're just a little local airfield here. We don't have any of that city stuff."

Mack stared at him, waiting to be recognised. It was Bob Albright, the man who had taught him to fly. But there was no sign of recollection in those bleary blue eyes.

Mack looked away, half disappointed, half relieved. Bob didn't remember him at all. But why should he? What Bob would remember was a teenage boy, eyes bright and full of interest and hope. What he saw before him now was one of the walking wounded—both literally and figuratively. His hair was just as black, but his face was twenty-four hours beyond the time it should have been shaven, and the scar left by the bullet that had ripped through his cheek five years ago in Colombia had never faded. His own sister wouldn't recognize him now. So why was he here?

Hell, he should haul his carcass out of here. What had he come for, anyway? He should get into the cockpit of his classic PBY and make tracks while the getting was good.

"Hey, mister, I'm going in to the crossroads. I can give you a lift."

Turning, he took in the presence of a youngster who reminded him of himself, twenty years ago—the same look of eager interest, the same greasy baseball cap, the same torn coveralls. It was obvious this one hung around cadging free flying lessons and offering to help anyone who would give them, just the way he had. The only difference was, this would-be pilot was a female.

"I'm not going all the way into town. Just out to the Taggert ranch."

Her dark eyes blinked and she shook her head. "Don't know that one."

"Small place. Does the name Tom Taggert ring a bell? Or..." Now this was a tough one, because the last time he'd seen her, she hadn't been married to Tom, and in his dreams, she never would have done it. "How about his wife, Taylor Taggert?"

"Oh. I think my mom knows her. But I'm still not sure..."

"It's right next to the Carlson place."

"Ah." She nodded happily. Everyone knew the huge Carlson place. "I'm going right past that. I'll drop you off." She grinned, a pixilated tomboy. "That is, if you don't mind riding on the back of a sickle. That's what I ride."

A motorcycle, at his advanced age, and with his bum leg, the result of a crash landing in the Bolivian jungle last year. He almost groaned aloud, but then he looked into the kid's bright eyes and held it back. "I guess I could handle that," he said instead.

"Great." She stuck out her ridiculously slim hand to shake his callused paw. "My name's Lani Tanaka. I'll get my stuff and we can go."

He hesitated, watching her dash away. She was so young, a part of the present here at the field. And he felt so very old. He was a part of the past. No one even remembered him. Taylor Taggert wasn't going to recognize him, either. Why not just leave? Why go through this?

"Are you ready?" She was back, bright eyed and impatient.

"Nope." His mouth twisted in half a grin. "But I'm going anyway."

He slung his flight bag over his shoulder and turned to follow her out to the road.

"Hey, take good care of my baby," he called out to the thin, bespectacled mechanic as he passed him in the doorway. "I'll be back tomorrow."

The young man turned and looked at him. "You the guy who flew in that restored PBY?" he asked, interest glinting in his hazel eyes. "Don't worry. I'll handle that beauty with kid gloves."

"I'd appreciate it," Mack answered, nodding before he swung away to follow Lani. That plane was all he had left in the world. All that he cared about, anyway.

He stopped short as Lani pulled out her "sickle." He hadn't exactly expected her to produce a hog, but neither had he expected something that looked like an aging bicycle with a battery pack.

"This is it," she said proudly.

"What? This piece of..." His gaze met Lani's wide-eyed innocence. Only a monster could hurt this kid. "This piece of excellent machinery," he improvised lamely. "Uh...this is it, huh?"

"This is it. I reconditioned it myself."

She kick started the thing and he had to admit, it hummed like a top. Still, he was going to feel ridiculous riding behind her on it. Sort of like those bears in the circus, riding tricycles.

She hopped astride. "Let's go," she said.

"Yeah, let's go," he muttered as he balanced himself and his bag precariously behind her. This was not the way he had pictured himself making an entrance at the Taggert place. Taylor was not going to be bowled over. More and more evidence was piling up to convince him—he should never have tried to come home.

If he hadn't been so overwhelmed by it all—the green hills, the soft trade winds in the trees, the scents and sounds he remembered so well—Taylor would never have gotten the drop on him the way she did. After all, he was an experienced agent of sorts. He'd come up against some pretty rough customers in his time. He knew how to react defensively.

But he'd been knocked out by the beauty, the softness in the air, and emotions had flooded him for a few moments as he walked in from the main road where he'd had Lani drop him off, past the plumerias and hibiscus that lined the path to the little house. Emotions were usually pretty deep with him. He didn't like to let them get too near the surface. But for just a moment, he'd stopped and turned slowly, taking it all in, remembering a past that could never be again, missing it, missing home and actually feeling a slight stinging in his eyes. And that was when she got him.

"Okay, you bastard, hold it right there. Don't make a move."

At the same moment the voice hit him, both barrels of a shotgun were jammed very hard and very painfully into the small of his back, and he groaned in disbelief. He hadn't even heard her coming up behind him. He was losing it.

"I'd like to blast a hole right through you. How would you like that, you slime ball?"

"Hey, hold on just a minute..."

The barrel jabbed him. "Don't try to talk, dirt bag. Just start walking. I'm going to walk you right off my land, and then I'm going to call the cops. And the next time you come slinking around I'm going to blow your brains out. You got that?" She jabbed him again to get him going toward the road. "And you can tell Bart Carlson I'll do the same for any other of his pathetic flunkies that he sends over here to screw up my life."

It took only one quick twist and a little leverage, and he had her on the ground, his big body holding hers down, the shotgun wrenched from her grasp and sent spinning in the dust.

But that didn't mean she gave up. Not by any means. She fought like a wildcat, spitting and scratching at him with fury. It took both his hands to hold down hers, and the full length of his body to hold her captive.

"Cut it out, Taylor," he growled at her, annoyed that she wasn't giving up even once she'd realized his superior strength. "I'm not going to hurt you."

The sound of her name was what seemed to still her for a moment. She stared up at him and he stared down at her, wondering if she had any idea that they had known each other before.

She'd changed. But her hair was still blond, still a mass of shimmering tangles that seemed to go on forever. Her body was still slim and lithe, but there was a strength to her he wouldn't have thought she would ever possess. She was still squirming beneath him, but it was beginning to feel good. He glanced at her cotton blouse, all askew and revealing the soft curve of her breast and a tiny strip of lace.

"Don't," she spat at him fiercely.

He looked up. Her face was older, naturally. The crystal blue eyes he remembered so vividly were wary, haunted by pain and struggle she couldn't have dreamed of in her younger days. And she wasn't laughing. In his memories, she was always laughing.

There was no sign of recognition. Didn't anybody remember him? Had he been erased from the consciousness of an entire community?

"I'll kill you if you go through with this," she warned, her voice low and full of menace despite her obvious disadvantage in her position beneath him on the grass.

He stared into her eyes. "Go through with what?" he asked softly.

She licked her dry lips. "Get off me, you bastard. Touch me and I'll make sure you're dead by..."

He winced. She was still thinking the worst of him, even when she didn't know who he was. "Relax, Taylor. I'm not going to rape you. I just want to make sure you're not going to shove a gun in my back again if I let you go."

A flicker of uncertainty appeared in her crystal eyes. She pulled back to see him more clearly. "Who *are* you?" she asked.

"Mack Caine," he said shortly. "The guy you hired to protect you. Remember?"

He could feel her tension seep away beneath him, and it was oddly pleasant. He knew it was time to let her up, but she felt so good. . . .

"Why didn't you say so?" she demanded, squirming unsuccessfully. "I expected you yesterday."

"I got detained." Got cold feet was more like it. He'd spent most of yesterday in a bar in San Francisco, using alcohol as a truth serum and trying to decide whether he really wanted to go through with this.

"I thought you were one of Bart Carlson's men," she explained shortly, but he noticed she didn't apologize for ramming the shotgun into his back. This was not the sweet girl he'd known in high school. This was a woman hardened and toughened by the years. Or maybe it was just the position she found herself in these days. After all, women didn't go hiring protection unless they were feeling really threatened.

"I figured you thought I was one of the bad guys," he said softly. "Do I really look like a bad guy to you?"

Silly that the answer to that question was so critical to him. But that was pretty much what he'd come for, wasn't it? If this place and its people still looked at him that way, there was hardly any point in going on with this.

She met his gaze and a slight frown creased the space between her sky blue eyes. She hesitated for a moment, then ignored the question.

"Are you going to let me up?" she demanded instead.

He didn't want to. She felt good beneath him. There was a hint of humor in his eyes as he looked at her. "I don't know. I kind of like this."

She struggled again. "Well, I don't. Let me up right now, you big oaf, or you're fired."

It almost made him laugh to think of this little thing ordering him around this way. He'd never worked for a woman before. This was going to take some adjusting.

He released her slowly, just so she wouldn't start thinking he was following orders or anything like that. She was hiring him, but he was reserving the right to quit anytime. He was going to have to make that clear to her. This wasn't like the old days. She wasn't nobility and he wasn't scum. If she couldn't face that, they were going to have a problem.

He rose, dusting off the knees of his jeans as he did so, and she rose as well. She stood with her hands on her hips and her face tilted at a challenging angle, looking him over. She was thinner than he'd remembered. Her light frame barely filled the colorful blouse and shorts set she wore. When she pushed her thick blond hair away from her face, the movement was quick, awkward, almost nervous.

"So you're Mack Caine, from Los Angeles," she said slowly, her gaze taking in all of him, her face blank and impersonal.

He twitched involuntarily. This was beginning to get very annoying. She really didn't know him. Didn't the name give her a clue? True, he hadn't gone by Mack in the old days. Still, the Caine was the same. "Yup, that's me."

Her blue eyes met his dark ones, searching for something she didn't seem to be finding. "Well, at least we know you can handle a five foot six woman with a shotgun," she said, just a hint of a barb to her tone.

He grinned. "Looks like. Though I haven't had much cause to. Until now."

"Haven't you?" She didn't seem convinced. "I suppose I should count that in your favor."

"You can count it any way you like." The humor faded from his eyes as he watched her rub her wrist. "I didn't hurt you, did I?" he asked quickly, taking a step forward.

"No." Her head went back and her eyes issued a warning. The message was unmistakable. He wasn't to come any closer. There had been about as much touching as there was ever going to be between them. "If I get hurt, I'll let you know."

"Good," he replied, backing off. "And I'll do the same."

Her gaze met his again, her brows slightly drawn, as though she'd noticed something familiar after all. Maybe she recalled something about his voice. He waited, almost holding his breath. She was going to recognize him any second now. And then what? Would she remember all the bad things about him? Would she order him off her land again? No, more likely she would be polite, tell him she'd forgotten, but the job was already filled. He waited, but she blinked, as though pushing away something that bothered her, and looked quickly around the yard.

"Where are your things?" she asked shortly, bending over to pick up the shotgun and let it lean against her leg, the barrel in the grass. "Are you planning to stay?"

"I left my bag by the road where my ride dropped me off."

"Ah." She turned and looked at him, letting her gaze run over the length of him, her expression full of skepticism. "I haven't hired you yet, you know. We still have some things to go over."

He opened his arms and shrugged. "Ask me anything. My life is an open book."

She threw him an "oh, please" look and said curtly, "Do you really think you can handle this job?"

He dropped his arms and grinned. "I wouldn't have come all this way if I didn't think that."

She nodded slowly. "You look pretty tough," she murmured, more to herself than to him. "You might do."

He felt a rush of adrenaline and he didn't know why. It tingled in his fingertips. She was going to hire him. He was going to stay here with her. But how long was it going to take her to realize who he was?

Two

Taylor was feeling an odd tingling, too, but hers was more like feminine intuition. She was probably going to have to hire this man. But she wasn't sure she was happy about it.

She glanced at him again. There was something about this Mack Caine that was tickling the edges of her mind. Where had she seen him before? And why did he keep looking at her that way?

She was feeling uncertain and she hated that. This was crazy. She shouldn't have done this at all. What did she know about him? She'd hired him, basically, by mail order. Did that mean, just as with any other mail order item, she could send him back? Of course. Just one little flaw would be enough for a return.

"How did you get here?" she asked curiously.

"I flew in. I've got my own prop job stashed at the airfield."

"Ah," she said again. That was good. If for any reason this product *did* turn out to be defective...

He was still looking at her strangely, and she remembered how he'd called her Taylor when he'd had her down on the grass a few moments earlier. She could put him in his place by requesting that he call her Mrs. Taggert. He'd been awfully free with her first name right from the start, and it would do him good to know she'd noticed. A tiny spark flashed in her eyes at the thought, but she dismissed it right away. She was pretty sure they were roughly the same age. She couldn't quite justify being that formal, even though it would have been comforting to put another wall between them.

Now, why had she thought that? She grimaced, annoyed with herself. There was nothing threatening about this man—nothing she couldn't handle, anyway. All she had to do was say something chilly to put him in his place, something to remind him of who was in charge here.

But he spoke next, before she had a chance to say anything. "Why don't you give me some sort of background on what this is all about?" he asked her, shifting his weight from one foot to the other.

She gazed at him uncertainly, as though she still didn't trust him enough to get into it. Her examination took in his wide shoulders and the air of wary competence that seemed to hang on him like the ancient leather bomber jacket he wore. His presence was strong and unambiguous. For just a moment, she hesitated. He wasn't going to be a man who was easy to control. She didn't want to set anything in motion that she couldn't handle. But then, when you came right down to it, she didn't really have much choice.

That meant she would have to be as tough as she possibly could be. She mustn't let him get the idea at any time that she was vulnerable. Unconsciously, she squared her shoulders. This wasn't going to be quite as easy as she'd thought.

Mack watched her eyes, waiting to catch the first flicker of recognition, but he didn't see a hint of it. Surely it would come eventually. Or had she never really paid enough attention to him to keep a small file in her memory banks? That thought had its own little sting, seeing as how his file on her was probably the biggest he had—other than the one he kept on Jill, anyway. And he was seriously considering shredding that one.

"Let's go into the house," she suggested. "You can see for miles from the front window. And we're an easy target out here in the open."

Mack's mouth twisted and he gave a quick, sweeping glance at the surroundings. "What...you expect your enemies to lob grenades in over the plumerias?" he asked, skepticism clear in his tone.

"I'm ready for anything," she told him quite seriously, starting for the house. "And you'd better be, too, if you're going to work for me."

Great. She was paranoid. Still pretty, but definitely over the edge. From what she'd told him on the phone, he'd figured out that Bart Carlson was the problem here. He knew Bart from the old days. The man was a jerk, but somehow Mack couldn't picture him in the part of jungle terrorist.

Turning, he followed her up the wide veranda steps and into the house. Inside, the place was surprisingly light and breezy. The rattan furniture he would have expected, but somehow the lacy white curtains fluttering in the afternoon trades seemed out of character for Taylor in her present metamorphosis as fierce defender of the fortress. Flowers—she had them everywhere, in pots, in jars, in glasses and vases. He was about to ask who had died when he realized that would have been in fairly poor taste, considering the fact that Tom seemed to have departed the premises, one way or another. But then again, he'd never been known for his tact.

Still, he managed to keep himself in check for the moment, dropping down to sit in the chair that she indicated for him across from the couch. He could hear a television going in the back of the house. Cartoons, it sounded like. Someone was back there. He looked at her, waiting, but she didn't say a word. And he damn well wasn't going to ask.

"Would you like something to drink?" she asked, managing to sound only grudgingly hospitable. "Beer, wine, juice..."

He winced, thinking of his long stint in the bar the day before. "Just something cold...iced tea or a soda would be great."

She nodded and turned toward the kitchen. He watched her disappear, her step as light as ever, her movements a little too quick, and he marveled at how this had happened, how he'd ended up here in Taylor's living room. Taking a deep breath, he steadied himself. Nope, he wasn't dreaming. This was for real.

Taylor Taggert. That was a new one on him. He'd always thought of her as Taylor Reynolds, her maiden name. And he'd been sure the T. Taggert in the ad he'd found in the Los Angeles newspaper was Tom Taggert, his old nemesis from high school days. He'd been certain of it when he'd dialed the number and waited for the call to go through to Hawaii. And then a woman had come on the line, saying, "Yes, I'm the T. Taggert in the ad. My name is Taylor." And he'd been stunned, momentarily rendered speechless. His entire body had gone numb, along with his brain. All he'd been able to do was stutter out his name, his basic qualifications and the fact that he wanted the job.

"Fine," she'd said. "I don't have time to mess around. Be here by Tuesday. If you pass the interview, you can start right away."

"What if I don't pass the interview?"

"Then you can't start right away. Am I going to have to add an I.Q. test to the process?"

He'd been dazed, unable to ask the right questions or identify himself to her. After all these years, there was Taylor on the other end of the phone line. Hiring him to come to her. It was too weird.

But once he hung up and thought it over, it was difficult to reconcile this brusque, no-nonsense Taylor with the sweet, golden girl he'd known in high school. Still, he knew she had to be one and the same. Taylor and Tom had been an item from the first, small-town royalty, high school style.

He'd been the other stereotype, the bad boy. The kind of boy sunshine girls like Taylor wouldn't touch with a ten-foot pole.

But Tom had been president of the senior class and star of the football team. And he'd married Taylor. Somehow that had never entered into Mack's memories of her. Whenever he'd imagined her, on lonely nights when he couldn't sleep, she'd been young and smiling and free—free for him to hold and to touch. Because that was the way it had always been, him dreaming, her laughing. He'd been an outsider to her small circle of select friends. Always on the outside, looking in.

But that was high school. That was long, long ago. Things were different now. He was grown up, and so was she. The time for dreams was over.

He was curious about what had happened. The closest he'd come to the core of the matter was in the original conversation when he'd asked if she would be hiring him herself or if he would be working for her husband.

"You'll work for me," she had said shortly. "There is no Mr. Taggert at the present time."

He hadn't spent much energy wondering about her marital status after that. If she was calling herself Taggert and living on the Taggert land, Tom had to be dead. Surely she wouldn't have held on to the place after a divorce. And even if she had, she probably wouldn't be calling herself Taggert.

He stretched in the chair and looked toward the kitchen, wishing she would hurry back. He needed to prove to himself that she was real.

Taylor was in the kitchen trying to steady her nerves with a slow drink of cold water. The man sitting in her living room was turning out to be more than she'd bargained for, and she was feeling shaky. But this was no time to fall apart. She'd done damn well since Tom had died—kept herself sane, turned the business around, held on to the land and done the best she could for Ryan, their son. And it hadn't been easy.

When she'd first lost Tom, she'd thought her life was over. They were married for twelve years. She didn't know anything else, couldn't imagine being with any other man, ever. Tom had been hers since high school. He'd been her rock, her reason for living—and sometimes her burden, as well. But he'd been hers, and when he'd died, her life seemed to fade into a pale nothingness.

For weeks she'd gone around in a fog, not sure what to do next. She'd thought about selling out and leaving Hawaii, trying to find a place without the memories. She'd called real estate agents. She'd made inquiries. But then one night Ryan had crawled into her lap and put his head against her shoulder and cried, the first time he had let his young mind really encompass the tragedy that had befallen his life. And when it was all over and they both were drying their tears, Ryan had said, "I'm going to grow up to be a rancher, just like Daddy. I'll take care of you, Mommy, just like he did." And it came to Taylor in a flash that she wouldn't leave. This ranch was Ryan's heritage. It was all he had left of his father. She couldn't take that away from him.

The fog had quickly burned away after that. She'd taken hold of the ranch and the business and made it better than it ever had been. She hadn't done it because she loved the work, but because she loved her son, loved him with a fierce, searing passion that wouldn't let her rest. This was his and she would preserve it for him. No one was going to change that.

That was why she'd been forced to hire outside help to counter Bart Carlson's land-grab attempt. That was why she was in the position of inviting Mack Caine to stay in her house and help her. She had to do what she had to do. Steeling herself, she picked up the two frosty glasses of iced tea and headed to the living room.

She sank down to sit stiffly at the edge of a pillow on the couch, trying to decide if she'd done the right thing hiring this stranger. It was a double-edged sword. He was very rough looking. That was a little scary. But at the same time, she needed rough looking. The point *was* to scare Bart and his crew. Would this man do that?

Well, he didn't look like a gangster. But his face was hard, and that scar running the length of one cheek made him look dangerous—like a man who had risked a lot in the past and might be willing to do so again. His movements were rather slow and lazy looking, but she had an idea that was a ruse. He'd moved quickly enough when he'd pinned her to the ground. He could take care of himself. But would he take care of her and hers?

"I guess we ought to get down to business," she said crisply, determined to keep a professional distance with body language as well as speech. "The first thing we should talk about is weapons."

He looked up from his tea, startled. To a man in his business, weapons were close and individual. Talking about them seemed almost too personal. "Weapons?" he repeated.

She nodded. "Did you bring your own, or will you need me to supply you with a gun?"

He shifted uncomfortably in his seat and stared into his glass. What did she think this was, the Old West? There was something off beam about this whole situation.

"I...I've got my own equipment," he said quickly. "I'm okay."

The knife in his boot and the Smith & Wesson strapped to his ribs had been enough to get him through the past ten years flying intercept missions with the DEA into South America, breaking up the drug trade. Surely they would be enough to see him through this little exercise in neighborhood push and shove. But just as surely, he didn't want to talk about them.

"You still haven't filled me in on just what we're facing here," he said, steering her away from the topic.

She set her glass of tea down very carefully, wiping up a bit of spilled water with her finger.

"We're a very small ranch," she said, staring at her hands. "This ranch has been in my husband's family for generations. And for generations, this place has existed in the shadow of a huge and very successful neighboring spread that belongs, at the moment, to a man named Bart Carlson."

She settled back against the cushions, glancing at him and then out the window at the palm fronds being ruffled by the breeze.

"There's never been any sort of trouble between the two ranches before. That I know of, anyway. But recently...well, things have changed." She turned her head and looked into his face. "Bart seems to want to push us out. He wants to add us to his long list of acquisitions. He's doing everything he can think of to scare me into selling."

Good old Bart, still throwing his weight around. "Why? What's changed?"

She hesitated, looking outside again. "I'm not sure. I've got two theories. First is the fact that the Kala River, which is one of their main water resources, flows right through a corner of our land before they get it. Bart may want firmer control. He once said something that made me think he might be leery about the future and his access to that water." She shook her head. "I don't think they ever thought that way when they were dealing with Tom . . . my husband. But now that I'm in charge, maybe he's nervous." She shrugged, searching Mack's dark eyes as though there might be a clue there.

"Then there's also our recent success," she went on. "The Taggert ranch was pretty much on a subsistence level for years, but lately I've lined up some new customers. We produce a special product—hormone-free beef that's been fed a specialized diet." A half smile flitted across her lips. "Real gourmet stuff. We get good money on it."

He nodded slowly. So she was a good businesswoman. Better without Tom than with him. Interesting.

"But that would put you out of direct competition with the Carlson beef, wouldn't it?"

"Yes." She sighed, looking suddenly tired. "Maybe he's just jealous. I don't know."

Mack looked her over. She wasn't a hysteric. He was pretty sure of that. There had to be something to all this anxiety. "So what is it that Carlson does to try to get you off the land?" he asked quietly.

"Well, let's see. Where to begin?" She began to tick off the bits of evidence on her fingers. "They've stampeded my cattle twice. They've burned down my bunkhouse. They've made threatening phone calls. They've caused two cowboys to quit and terrified Josi, our wrangler, who's been with us since time immemorial and is in his eighties now. They've tried to pressure my suppliers to quit selling me feed. They've tried to pressure my customers into dropping my accounts."

Mack nodded. "How do you know Carlson is behind it?"

"Because there's no one else it could possibly be." She took a deep breath. "And because every time something happens, he's on my doorstep in moments, full of sympathy and promises to help—and offers to buy me out. For my own peace of mind, of course."

"Ah, I see." He tried to remember what Bart Carlson looked like. Tall, brown hair, sort of a permanent sneer, if he remembered correctly. "Bad cop, good cop."

"Sort of."

"And what about the real cops?"

She looked at him wearily. "The police come out and make reports and go away again. I tried to hire local private cops, but they all take orders from Bart. I didn't know what else to do. I put an ad in the Los Angeles paper and hoped for the best."

"And you got me." Mack laughed shortly. "I don't know if I'm the best, but I'll do what I can."

Her eyes were clear, her chin high and defiant. "I don't know how bad it will get," she warned.

He sobered. Something about her bravery touched him. "Don't worry, Taylor. I can handle bad."

She nodded slowly as though she believed him. Still, her next words didn't show complete confidence.

"You're not quite what I expected," she said softly, looking him over again.

He felt like an insect being pinned to the wall. "What did you expect?"

"I don't know. Someone older, maybe...more like a cop."

Who was she trying to kid? She almost laughed at herself. The older wasn't the point, and neither was the cop comment. What she'd expected was someone a little less attractive, a little less dangerous. To her peace of mind, at any rate. Because no matter how much she tried to tell herself he wasn't going to bother her, she knew it wasn't true. She'd already felt a stirring of interest, so she knew she was going to have to fight it. And then there was the way he kept looking at her, and the strange feeling she kept getting that she'd seen him before.

"What you see is what you get," he said in response to her observation.

She looked at him again, noting the large hands, the strong fingers. A tiny shiver ran the length of her spine and she bit her lip. What she was buying here was a very large and powerful weapon. She only hoped she was going to have the ability to control it.

"Are you married?" she asked formally, picking up a ledger book from the table and opening it to a page where she began to jot down notes.

"I was."

"What happened?"

He didn't answer right away, and she let the pencil pause in the air and looked at him questioningly.

"She's married to someone else now." He said it warily, like a man expecting the worst, and then he waited for the pain that was usually associated with bringing Jill into his mind. But somehow it didn't come this time. There was just a dullness, a void. He looked at Taylor in surprise, wondering why.

She stared at him for a moment, then reached into the book and pulled out a paper with some figures on it. After glancing at it for a moment, she handed it to him.

"This is what you'll get if I hire you. Bear in mind you get room and board here. It's a twenty-four-hour job."

"And how long do you expect to need me?"

She shrugged. "Hopefully, not much longer than a few weeks. Long enough for Bart to get the message that I'll do anything I have to do to hold on to this land." She reminded him quickly, "That is, if I hire you."

He nodded slowly, eyes glinting. "Tell me something," he drawled. "Have you had many applicants for this job?"

He was the only one. He could see it in her eyes. But she wouldn't admit it.

"That is none of your concern," she snapped. "Let's stick to the issue of your qualifications."

He grinned. He couldn't help it. "Whatever you say, boss," he murmured, chuckling.

She flushed, but before she could tell him what she thought of his sense of humor, a door opened at the other end of the house and a young boy who looked about six years old began to come slowly toward them, his feet scuffing noisily. She turned and all her sternness fell away, revealing a smile Mack hadn't seen except in dreams for a long, long time. *There* was the Taylor he knew. It was a relief to know she still existed.

Taylor beckoned for the boy to come a little faster, and when he arrived, she pulled him into the circle of her arm. From that vantage, he glared at Mack, making it very clear he considered him an intruder.

"Ryan, this is Mr. Caine. He's going to help us for a while. Would you shake hands with him, please?"

The boy did as he was ordered, but he took no pleasure in it. A telephone rang from somewhere in the back of the house. Taylor jumped up.

"Darn," she muttered. "That's got to be a call from a supplier I've been expecting. You'll have to excuse me for a moment. Ryan, you keep Mr. Caine company." And, throwing them a distracted look, Taylor turned away and left the room to answer the call.

Ryan stood where his mother had left him and stared at Mack, and Mack stared back in wonder. The kid was an exact replica of Tom, only smaller, and redheaded instead of blond. He had the same piercing gray eyes, the same firm chin, the same skinny legs. Amazing.

He supposed it was up to him, as the adult, to break the ice. "So, Ryan," he tried heartily. "How's it going?"

Ryan's brows came down even further over his eyes. "My dad was bigger than you," he stated clearly in a voice that could have carried out to the highway.

Mack blinked. His own six foot two frame was nothing to sneeze at. "Then he must have grown a lot after high school," he muttered under his breath.

Such heresy did not deter the boy. His eyes narrowed. "My dad was smarter than you," he announced just as firmly.

Mack shrugged. "That I can believe."

Ryan sneered. "My dad was braver. And he used to win the bucking contest at the rodeo, too."

Mack nodded slowly. "You got me there," he admitted good-naturedly. "Rodeos never were my strong suit."

"My dad was...was...was handsomer than you."

Mack grinned. "And you look just like him."

That surprised him. His eyes widened for a moment and he let out an automatic "I know I do." There was no answering smile, but the comment seemed to throw him off his stride and he didn't go on with the comparisons.

"I used to know your dad," Mack told him gently. "In fact, we used to do favors for each other sometimes."

Ryan blinked his big gray eyes. "Was he your friend?"

Mack hesitated. What would a little lie hurt now? "Sure, Ryan. We were friends." In an odd sort of way it might even be true. At least from the safe vantage point of history. He couldn't claim they'd ever liked one another. But they had done a few things together. Didn't that count?

Ryan nodded, as though he'd been sure of that all along. He turned to go to his room, but looked back with one last message, glaring again. "Don't try to kiss my mom, okay?"

Mack's jaw dropped. "What?"

The glare was piercing. "There's a man that tries to kiss her. I had to hit him last time."

Mack swallowed and shook his head. A part of him would have loved to have seen that little scene played out. "Listen, Ryan, I'm not here to kiss your mom, honest. I'm just here to help you and her protect what you own. That's all."

Ryan stared at him for a moment longer, then turned and disappeared down the hall. Mack took a deep breath and gave a short laugh. Kissing.

No, kissing was not in his plans. He hadn't come to do any kissing. In fact, he'd come for quite the opposite.

It was true memories of Taylor hadn't hurt, but they certainly weren't what had brought him across the ocean. This had been home once. For too long, he'd tried to ignore that. He'd tried to make a new home with Jill, and for years he thought he'd succeeded, that he didn't need Hawaii anymore. But now that safe harbor was closed to him, shattered, defiled. And he found he needed something to anchor to. Thoughts of home, of his sister Shawnee, of Hawaii and his younger self began to haunt him. And when he'd seen the ad in the paper, it had all seemed to come together. If there was anything left for him here, he had to find it. He needed something. He hoped this was it.

Taylor was going to hire him. That much was obvious. She didn't have much choice. And if that was the case, he might as well get his bag in from the road before someone spotted it and took off with all his belongings. He rose from his seat just as she returned to the room.

"Where are you going?" she asked, but he didn't answer that. Instead, he looked at her, hard, and said, "What happened to Tom?"

She glanced toward Ryan's room and saw that the door was closed. "He's dead," she returned bluntly, not wasting any time on sentiment. "He died almost a year ago." She didn't go into details, but one eyebrow rose in question. "Did you know him?"

He nodded slowly. "Yes."

She was gazing at him curiously, and he wondered if she would begin to remember. Or did she remember him at all? He probably hadn't said twenty words to her before in his life. Maybe his existence had never penetrated her consciousness the way hers had devoured his. Maybe she'd thought he was a creep. Maybe she'd been happy to forget him as soon as he'd disappeared from her life.

"When did you know Tom?" she asked.

He hesitated, but somehow he couldn't just come out and tell her. "It was a long time ago," he said evasively. "I'll tell you about it sometime."

She didn't push, though he could see she wanted to.

Turning, he headed for the door. "I'm going out to the road to get my bag," he called over his shoulder. "I'll be right back."

Going to the door, she watched him swing down off the porch. He glanced over his shoulder, and his gaze met hers for a fleeting second, and in that same second, a sudden picture froze in her mind. It was an image of a younger man looking over his shoulder in that same way. The edges of the picture were gray and blurry, but the center was crystal clear. High school. She was in trig class, sitting at her usual desk, and the boy was a few rows up. He turned his dark head and looked at her. His gaze caught hers and held for one long moment.

For some crazy reason it was a moment that had returned to her periodically through the years. She'd never forgotten it, never forgotten those dark eyes. And suddenly she remembered something important. Those dark eyes belonged to a boy named Kimo Caine. And those same dark eyes now belonged to this man who was calling himself Mack.

"What in the world is going on here?" she whispered, her fingers to her lips as she watched him disappear around the hibiscus hedge. Kimo Caine, the black sheep, the town bad boy, the kid who had been in so much trouble that he'd left the island and never come back. Why was he really here? "What in the world is going on?"

Three

The sun was shining brightly, but a small cloud came over and dropped a quick rain shower, so warm and gentle it was hardly noticeable. Ordinarily she wouldn't have paid any attention. But this time, it worried her, as though it were some sort of magic rain, to wash away the last half hour, to wash away some crazy dream she'd been having. Kimo Caine. Had she been imagining things? Was he gone now?

But no. He was back in moments. She was still standing at the door, still stunned. Her heart was pounding. Why hadn't he told her who he was? Yes, as he came closer, she could tell it was definitely him. The long, slender, sinewy boy had been replaced by a larger, thick man. But the eyes were the same.

She stepped back and let him in. He dropped his duffel bag on the floor and turned to her with a smile, shaking the silver drops from his black hair.

"Liquid sunshine. Isn't that what you all call it here?"

"You should know," she wanted to say. Instead, she set her mouth in a grim line and nodded.

She was wary and perplexed. What strange twists life kept handing her. How in the world had this happened? He looked so very different from that smart-alecky boy she remembered so well. And his name hadn't been Mack. Kimo was what they all called him in those days. Kimo Caine. The wild boy of Paukai High.

"That's one of the Caines. They're descended from pirates, you know," her mother used to say when they would see him hanging around town. She would note the furtive glance Taylor would take, hoping to catch his dark eyes, curious to see what a boy descended from pirates was up to. "Those Caine kids are all wild. You stay away from that one, Tay. He's no good."

And it turned out she was right, as they all found out in their senior year when everything fell apart. He was no good. He'd skipped town just ahead of the proverbial law. And here he was, planning on protecting her.

How strange that he hadn't identified himself right away. She wasn't sure what he was up to, but if he thought he was going to pull something over on her, he had another think coming.

"Come on in and sit down, Mr. Mack Caine," she said evenly. "I have a few more questions to ask you."

This time she indicated a straight-backed chair in the middle of the room, and once he'd lowered himself onto it, she began to pace back and forth, making a circle around where he sat. She felt like a grand inquisitor. And more than that, she felt angry. She didn't like being made a fool of.

Mack sat watching her, noting that her manner had changed. He wasn't sure what it was that had caused it. Maybe the telephone call she'd taken? Maybe Ryan had said something to her. Whatever, her whole manner had taken on a new, harsher edge. The old Taylor could never have sustained it. This new Taylor seemed to wear it like a well-worn glove. He wasn't sure if this new cross-examination was just going to be routine, or if she had some trick questions in mind. He would have to be careful.

"How long has it been since your last job?" she was asking crisply.

"A few months."

"Why haven't you been working?"

"Burnout. I needed to recharge my batteries."

Her mouth twisted as though she didn't believe a word he said. "Is this your first trip to Hawaii?" she fired at him.

He was getting dizzy trying to follow her moves as she paced back and forth. But he enjoyed watching her, her bare legs smooth and tan, her figure trim in the shorts and top. "Uh…trip to Hawaii, yeah." That was true enough, as far as it went.

She stopped and glared at him. "I mean, have you ever been here before?"

He blinked. The correct answer to that would bring up all sorts of questions he wasn't sure he was ready for. "Why? Does it make a difference?"

Her eyes flashed as though she'd caught him out. "Maybe. That depends." She stood before him with her hands on her hips.

His eyelids drooped as he studied her stance. What was bugging this woman? "Is it going to be a factor in whether I get hired or not?"

She was tapping her foot. "Could be."

He tried a slow smile. "So what's the magic answer? Which one will get me the job?"

Her eyes blazed and she pointed an accusing finger at him. "Are you saying that what you're telling me is only true when it fits what you think I want to hear?"

He groaned, rolling his head back. "No. Listen, this is a job interview, not a trial for murder. Lighten up, for God's sake."

Lighten up? Taylor felt her shoulders sag. Who did this man think he was? "Oh, you want a regular job interview, do you?"

"That would be nice."

"Okay. Okay." She could play that game. She thought for a moment, then looked at him again. "If you were a tree, what kind of tree would you be?"

His laugh was short and incredulous. "What?"

She had to steel herself against his smile. It was infectious, and she didn't want to break down and like him. "That's an established interrogative technique," she said defensively. "Come on. What kind of tree would you be?"

He shook his head, amusement shining in his eyes. "I see. It's a way to try to get in to the deep hidden wellsprings of my soul and reveal character. Is that it?"

She gazed back defiantly. "Hopefully."

"Okay. I'll tell you what kind of tree I'd like to be." He frowned, thinking. "Okay, I've got it. I don't want to be a tree. I'd rather be a tumbleweed. That way I wouldn't have to have anybody nourishing my roots and I could just roll around anywhere I felt like going." He sat back, feeling very proud of himself.

Her anger was ebbing away. This was Kimo Caine, all right. And he'd always been outrageous. "Typical male response," she muttered, looking away so she wouldn't smile.

He grinned at her. "Do you find me typical?" he asked softly.

She glanced into his eyes and almost had to laugh. No, typical wasn't the right word for him. "I find you very male," she admitted grudgingly.

His grin broadened and an element of sensuality crept into his look. Leaning back, he hooked an arm over the top of the chair. "Well, that's a relief."

She shook her head, still staring into those dark eyes, finding it impossible to look away. "Were you worried?"

"No." His eyes were laughing. "I just want you to understand that I'm always ready with evidence should you require reassurance on that score."

Her heart was beating a little faster. This was insane. She was supposed to be mad at him, but she couldn't look away. "I don't think that will be a problem," she said, trying hard not to sound breathless. How had they gotten sidetracked down this crazy path? She finally found the strength to turn away. She had to or she would be smiling right into his face and he would have won. He was really impossible. Just like in the old days. But she had to get on with this. And there was still this matter of him hiding who he was. Turning back, she managed to keep a straight face.

"So tell me, Mr. Caine, what made you decide to come to Hawaii?"

"I needed a job."

"Okay. So you just opened a newspaper and saw the ad and thought, 'Gee, wouldn't it be fun to take a vacation in the islands'?"

He shifted in the chair. "Not exactly. I thought, 'Gee, I'm not working right now and I could use this job.'"

"Yes, but why this job? Why here?"

"I don't know. I just got the urge to try Hawaii for a change. Is that so strange?"

Maybe not strange. But it certainly was a coincidence. She sniffed and began to pace again. "Tell me once more about all your years with the government."

He shifted in the chair, looking at ease with the world. Nothing seemed to ruffle him for long. "It was contract work. I flew intercept missions for the interdiction arm of the DEA in South America.''

She turned and skewered him with a sharp glance. "Why did you quit that?''

He moved uncomfortably again. She was getting too close to the bone, too close to the part of his life he would rather forget. "I decided I didn't want to get killed, after all.''

That stopped her in her tracks. She stared at him, suddenly realizing he wasn't kidding this time. "What made you go ahead and take another dangerous job, then?''

"Dangerous?'' His mouth smiled but his eyes didn't. "Anybody been killed around here lately?''

"No, but...''

"I think I can handle the risk.'' He hesitated. She really deserved a better explanation. "The attrition rate in my old job began to get to me.'' He shrugged. "I figured I'd already got about as much help from the odds as I deserved. I don't like to push my luck.''

If he meant to appeal to her emotions, it was working. She couldn't help it. He was a human being, wasn't he? To think of him risking his life was oddly thrilling, and appalling at the same time. "It looks like you might have pushed it once or twice too often as it is,'' she noted softly, glancing at the scar that disfigured his cheek.

His fingertips barely touched the scar, almost as if to hide it from her gaze, but he smiled. "I've got better evidence than that, if you're interested,'' he said, and suddenly the twinkle was back in his eyes. "Evidence in certain covered areas that would require...''

"That's all right,'' she said hastily. "I'll take your word for it.''

"Finally, you trust me on something,'' he said softly.

She hesitated, her gaze caught by his. She was really going to have to fight this urge to let his natural male allure take over. Funny. She'd never had a problem with male authority before. She'd always held her own, never been intimidated. But there was something about this man...

Okay. She was tough. She could do it. Enough playing around. It was time to go in for the kill.

"Now tell me, Mr. Mack Caine," she said, enunciating every syllable, "just why was it that you decided to change your name?"

His face was blank and he didn't blink. "Change my name?"

So he wasn't going to come clean right off the bat. She stared at him for a moment, letting him twist in the wind, letting him study her face with that puzzled look. "Yes. Change your name," she said at last. "Care to elaborate?"

His dark eyes were wary, but there was a look of anticipation about him, too. "I don't know what you're talking about," he said softly. "I haven't changed my name."

"Oh, really?" She couldn't keep a note of triumph out of her voice. She stood square in front of him and glared. "It seems to me we used to call you Kimo in the old days."

A slow grin curled lazily across his face. It was incredible how happy it made him that she hadn't forgotten, after all. Ridiculous, really. "I thought you didn't remember me."

That grin was lethal. She had to steel herself not to let it get to her. "I remember you, all right."

Yes, she remembered. The more she watched him, the more the memories came pouring back. She remembered the hooded looks, the burning feeling when his gaze would slip over her, the way her breath would run ragged when she was too close to him. He'd intrigued her. She now realized he'd had a smoldering sexuality that had scared her at the time, made her shy away from him. He still had that. And he was still too dangerous to play around with. But she was older now and had seen a few things, been around. She could handle the pressure.

Mack was still grinning. "I was wondering how long it would take you to remember. You were starting to hurt my feelings."

She bit her lip and held back what she wanted to feel. He was very wily. He had a way of making you feel he cared and thought only about you. She'd seen him in action in the old days. It was a ploy she would never let herself fall for. Instead, she raised an eyebrow. "And I was wondering how long it would take you to come clean with the truth."

"I didn't lie to you."

"An omission is as bad as a lie."

He shook his head. "I get accused of enough without that," he protested. "I'm not a liar, Taylor. I'll never lie to you."

The seeming sincerity in his voice caught at her in a way she hadn't expected. There seemed to be something choking her throat. She cleared it, avoiding his gaze. "But you still haven't answered the question," she reminded him. "Why the name change?"

"There was no name change. Kimo was my nickname then. Mack's my nickname now. The real name is and always has been MacKenzie. After my maternal grandfather."

That's right. She remembered that now. And she remembered something else. "You had a sister," she said, changing the subject just a bit.

He nodded, his face impassive. "Shawnee."

"Shawnee. That was her name. I haven't seen her in years."

"Neither have I."

There was a note of wistful regret in his voice. She glanced at him quickly, but his face was still a blank. Maybe she'd imagined it. After all, bad boy Caine from her teenage years wouldn't be the type to regret anything. He was too tough, too cool, too careless. And that brought up another question. He'd been gone all these years. Why had he chosen this time to come back?

She put a hand to her forehead and took a deep breath. She had to stop this. She couldn't get too personal here. If she got personal, she would end up involved in his personal life, and that was something she didn't want to do. She felt a real temptation, though. There was something deep inside her that wanted to reach out to him. Was it because he represented a safe and distant past? No, that couldn't be it, because he had never been safe. That was one thing about Kimo Caine—he'd been the most dangerous boy she'd ever known.

He stood, suddenly, and faced her, his thumbs hooked into his wide leather belt, his head cocked. "So what's it going to be, boss lady?" he asked her. "Do I get the job?"

She knew she had no choice, but she couldn't bear to give in completely. "I guess I could put you on probation for a few days," she said, chin high. "Just to see if you work out."

He laughed, his eyes crackling with impudent humor. "Call it what you will, Taylor. You wanted a hired gun, and you got one." He gave her a mock bow. "Mack Caine, at your command."

At your command. She sort of liked the sound of that. But she wouldn't admit it. "We'll see" was all she would give him.

She was still apprehensive. This was, after all, the man who had been the boy everyone had talked about, the boy who was said to be behind everything bad that happened, the boy a mother wouldn't let her daughter date, the boy a father wouldn't let his son hang out with. Descended from pirates. And here she was, hiring him, bringing him into her family. Was she nuts? Or very, very crafty?

Did he remember how she would stare at him in trig, guiltily fascinated by his dark good looks, puzzled at how easy learning was for him and how carelessly he threw away the grade by stubbornly refusing to follow the rules? She hoped not, because he certainly didn't seem to have improved over the years. She was glad she had loved and married Tom. For all his faults, he had always tried so hard. And Mack—he was as attractive, as talented and as careless as ever. Pity the poor woman who fell in love with him. He was like a great wildcat who might lie by your side and purr for now, but whose wildness never quite left his eyes.

"So what exactly do you want me to do here?" he asked restlessly. "Patrol the perimeter? Stand guard all night? Go after the bastards in their own backyard?"

"That wasn't quite what I had in mind." She sank down onto the couch and he sank down beside her instead of going to the chair where she'd put him before. She noted the change, but decided not to fight it for the moment. She was too involved in trying to get across to him just exactly what her plan was. "When you come right down to it, I don't really want to do anything to them. I hate violence. I don't like hurting people."

He laughed shortly. "You could have fooled me," he muttered, ruefully rubbing the small of his back.

"Well, when push comes to shove, I'll defend myself and my property," she told him stoutly. "But I don't want to provoke anything. Actually...well, I want you here more as a deterrent than anything else."

"A deterrent?" He frowned. He was a man of action. This didn't really sound like his kind of work.

"I want your name spread all over town. I want everyone to know you're here, that you're prepared to do whatever it takes. I want you known, but I don't necessarily want you to do anything. Unless something happens and you have to."

He had mixed feelings about that. He liked to get in and get his hands dirty, direct action, act and not react. And there was another drawback to her plan. If his name was bandied about town, pretty soon his family was bound to hear about it. But maybe that was for the best. Who knew, maybe after all these years, they'd forgotten him, too. Hell, no one remembered. Except Taylor.

Then he realized the implications of what she was talking about. "Wait a minute. You want to tell people that I'm staying here with you?"

"You've got it."

His eyes narrowed as he gazed at her. Didn't she remember how it was? Didn't she remember who he was? He hesitated, then had to remind her. "You know, Taylor, if people do remember me, they're going to wonder what a nice girl like you is doing having me around."

She knew that. "Because of your reputation?" she asked softly.

He nodded, his eyes troubled.

Her smile was sunny. She was way ahead of him. She'd already thought this through. "Don't you get it? Your reputation is supposed to be part of the deterrent. You being considered such a villain will be the best part of it all."

He stared at her, not sure if he should be pleased or offended. What had just happened here? The world had done a flip-flop. Everything that used to be bad was good, and everything that used to be good was bad. He wasn't sure he liked it this way. He had his problems with the old system, but this new way of thinking was just too confusing. Especially since he'd been determined to come back and prove to everyone that they had been wrong about him in the first place.

But Taylor wasn't interested in things like that. She was bright eyed and ready to get on with it. "The best thing to do would be to get started right away."

"Get started?" His eyes took on a wary look.

"Yes. I'll grab Ryan, we'll go into town. . . ."

"Into town?" he repeated, thinking of his childhood home along the coast.

"Not really to town, not out to Paukai where you used to live. Just to the crossroads. It's been built up a bit over the last few years, and that's where the people are who need to know about you. That's where I need to put the message out."

Mack reached up and rubbed the back of his neck. It was feeling stiff, just like it always did when he was being dragged into something against his better judgment. "How do you know the message will get where you want it to go?"

Taylor had no doubts. She pushed her hair back with an impatient gesture, ready to sail into the future. "Bart has his spies everywhere. Half the people around here are beholden to him, one way or another. And Bart himself is always around."

Mack shrugged, giving in. "If this is what you want..."

"It's what I need," she sang out, starting away. "I'll get Ryan and we can get right on it."

She left the room in a whirl, but he didn't move. He stayed right where he was, sitting stock-still. He'd come home to clear his name and get rid of the bad reputation that had forced him to leave years ago. But now that he was here, he found that his reputation was his currency for sticking around. And like any trapped animal, his first inclination was to fight back.

A memory suddenly flashed into his mind, something he hadn't thought about for years. It was the homecoming dance, the fall of his senior year. Taylor hadn't been the homecoming queen, but she'd been one of the princesses. He hadn't been allowed to go to the dance because his student body card had been confiscated by the administration for some offense he couldn't remember now. He and a few of his buddies had been hanging around the entrance to the gym, watching the couples going in, calling out good-natured insults, pretending they weren't jealous, pretending they didn't wish they were going in, too, all dressed up with beautiful girls by their sides. A long, low white Chevy had driven up. Tom had jumped out and come around to open the door for Taylor. As she emerged, Mack felt as though he couldn't breathe. She was so beautiful, dressed in white lace and tiny violet flowers, her golden hair piled high in ringlets. Time stood still as he stared at her.

But it only stood still for him. The kid he was rough-housing with didn't get the picture, didn't realize Mack's attention was totally absorbed. His sucker punch to Mack's jaw, a punch he fully expected Mack to parry and avoid, landed, instead, square on target, and Mack went flying backward, slicing right through the huge banner that had been put up for the dance. He lay stunned, paper flapping around him, and suddenly there was Taylor leaning over him.

"Are you okay?" she was asking with true concern in her eyes.

For a moment, he wasn't sure where he was or what had happened. He only knew the most beautiful girl on earth was hovering over him, just in reach. Still groggy, he reached for her. All he wanted in the world was to take her in his arms and hold her. But before he could do that, Tom had yanked her away.

"Keep your hands off her, druggie," he'd snarled.

The scorn he'd seen in Tom's face had rankled. It still rankled. And worse was the question in Taylor's eyes as Tom hurried her away from the distasteful sight.

His first instinct had been to jump up and grab Tom and beat him to a bloody pulp. But he knew he couldn't do that. He was bright enough to understand that doing such a thing would only be filling in the spaces in the stereotype.

He'd come up slowly, filled with frustrated rage. No matter what he did, it always looked bad. But he wasn't a druggie. He never took drugs, not then, not ever. He hated drugs, hated what they'd done to people he knew, hated what he saw them doing to the country. Still, he had that damned reputation. Girls like Taylor were forever out of his reach. And that just made him want her more.

"Color me bad, ladies and gentlemen," he remembered whispering to himself that night. "Color me hopeless."

Four

—

Racing down the highway with the wind in her hair, Taylor felt excited, and she wasn't sure if it was because she was finally doing something to fight back against Bart Carlson or if it had more to do with the man sitting in the front seat beside her. At this point, she hardly cared. It had been a long time since she'd felt a man notice her, felt his awareness of her body, her hair, her lips. She felt it now, and though it scared her a little, it excited her, too. She was a widow, a mother and bound and determined not to fall for that hoax called romance, but she was still a woman. And it felt good to be noticed.

They stopped first to drop Ryan off at the home of a playmate. The house was a low ranch style set between nicely manicured lawns and a sparkling swimming pool.

"Run on in, Ryan," Taylor told her son, leaning across to open his door. "I'll be coming right behind you."

Ryan opened the car door, gave Mack a baleful look, as though he didn't know if he should trust him alone with his mother, and slowly slid out of the car.

"Go on, honey. Trent is waiting for you. Sue said he got his water slide fixed."

The boy's eyes didn't light up, but his feet began to move a little faster along the gravel driveway. Taylor waited until he was out of earshot, running for the front steps, and then she turned to look at Mack. This was only going to work if he cooperated.

"You just get out and kind of lean against the car. Okay?"

He stared at her. "What?" he asked, sure he couldn't have heard right.

But she was earnest. "Just sort of lean, you know what I mean. Look masculine."

She gave him a quick once-over and she had to squelch the little shivers that wanted to start running down her spine. He wasn't going to have to worry too much about that masculine bit. The man exuded something male that seemed to fill the air. She smiled at him. "Just be yourself," she added with a short laugh.

He caught the look, and it triggered a sense of surprise that he immediately suppressed. This was Taylor here, the girl who had scorned him in high school, the woman who had married Tom Taggert, his longtime nemesis. He wasn't going to fall into that trap again.

Still slightly mystified by what she wanted from him, but eminently obliging, he slipped out of the car and sauntered around to the front of the vehicle. "Sure, boss. Whatever you say."

She watched him take up his position, and it happened again—little tiny shivers. She almost had to laugh. There was going to be none of that! Shaking herself, she got out of the car, and started for the house.

"Lean nice," she called back in a stage whisper as she hurried away. "Look rough."

"Lean nice and look rough," he muttered, planting his rear end against the fender and folding his arms across his chest. "I'm not sure this woman speaks the same language as the rest of us."

But she threw him an approving smile as she hit the top step of the porch, so he supposed he was doing something right.

"Sue?" she called, looking into the house.

"Hi, Taylor." Sue was tall and model thin and always wore fashionable clothes, even for gardening. She'd grown up in New York City and had come to the islands in her late twenties with her ways already set. "Come on in."

Usually, Taylor would have done just that and the two of them might have shared some coffee or lemonade for a few moments, discussing their children and their respective lives. But not today. Taylor had something else in mind. She stayed where she was in the doorway.

"Sue, you come on out here and look at this."

Sue came to the door, her black hair swept up in a stylish do, her violet eyes sleepy. "What's up, darling?"

"I want you to see this." Taylor waved a hand toward where Mack was leaning. "What do you think?"

Sue's carefully cultivated ennui evaporated. Her eyes widened. "Ohmigosh. Who is *that?*"

Taylor grinned smugly and her eyes sparkled. "He's mine."

"Yours?" Sue made a sensual sound low in her throat. "Whatever do you mean?"

Taylor laughed. She was enjoying this much more than she'd expected. "His name's Mack Caine. I hired him."

Sue gasped dramatically and gave her a sweeping look. "To do what?"

She smiled, delaying her answer just long enough to make Sue reach out and shake her arm in her impatience to hear. "Protection."

Sue's look sharpened and she drew back. Taylor could see her visibly erecting defenses. "You're kidding, Taylor," she said coolly. "What on earth do you need protection from?"

Taylor set her jaw and held Sue's gaze. "Bart Carlson."

"What?" Something wary flickered in Sue's eyes, and Taylor knew why. Her husband worked for Bart. Sue was always defending him, excusing the rotten things he did, explaining how the man was misunderstood—trying to change Taylor's mind about him. It would be interesting to see how she handled this news. But more than that, this was exactly what Taylor wanted, a direct pipeline to Bart himself.

"Bart's been pressuring me to sell. You know that. I finally decided I needed a man to support me. So I hired one."

Sue stared at her for a long moment without commenting, then went back to staring at Mack. Taylor could almost see her mind working, deciding to avoid direct confrontation over the issue, planning to notify Bart right away.

"He sure is a man, all right," Sue drawled, looking him over. "I guess you might be getting your money's worth." She chuckled and looked at Taylor again. "Let me know when you're through with him. I could use some of that kind of protection myself."

Taylor let out a long sigh. She'd planted the seed. Her work here was done. She turned to go, looking back only to throw out another zinger. "He's a hired gunman, Sue. Think you could handle that?"

Sue was speechless and Taylor was feeling smug again. "Well, see you later. I'm just going to the crossroads to do some shopping. I'll be back to get Ryan about five. Okay?"

"Okay," Sue said dully, watching her go.

"Thanks," Taylor called as she hurried to the car.

Funny, but she really did consider Sue a friend. Ryan and Trent played together all the time, either at Sue's place or at Taylor's. But Sue and her husband were close to Bart, and that had become a problem lately.

"You can stop leaning now," she said to Mack as she whipped past him. "You did a great job."

"Thanks," he muttered wryly, straightening and turning to watch her. "It's so good to have your work appreciated."

He swung into the car beside her and soon they were off down the gravel road, heading toward the highway.

"Ten to one she's on the phone to Bart right now," Taylor chortled. "Next stop, the country store."

Mack shook his head. It was interesting watching her work. She was completely involved in this scheme of hers, full of energy and excitement. He didn't remember her this way. But then, his memories were of a girl, not a woman. She'd changed.

He pondered her profile for a moment. That hadn't changed at all. He'd always thought she looked like an angel, her face so perfect, her body so light, her hair like a blond halo around her head. It felt strange letting her drive. He was used to being the one in charge, and this felt like giving up a bit too much of the initiative. But she was the boss. He was going to have to keep reminding himself of that.

Another thing bothered him. He was going along with this "reputation" stuff for now, but he didn't much like it. Using it ran counter to his whole purpose in being here. He wanted to fight that image, renovate it. It was based on half-truths, anyway. He really didn't deserve it.

But what was he supposed to do and how was he supposed to do it? He couldn't very well just interject it casually into the general conversation. "Oh, by the way, you know how you used to think I was a young crook in the old days? Well, you were dead wrong. Honest. I was really a good kid. I just looked bad."

Stunning speech. She would probably applaud with a tear in her eye, and he could go on his way secure in the knowledge that she now knew the truth. Right.

He'd come to prove something to everyone who'd known him when he was young, everyone who'd been so sure he was no good. Right now, that was beginning to mean proving it to Taylor. And in proving it to Taylor, he would prepare himself to prove it to his sister. Shawnee was the main reason he had left home so many years ago, and she was the main reason he had come back now.

"Tell me something. Is that going to be the substance of my job?" he asked, stretching out as well as he could in her little car. "Am I going to be leaning on cars a lot?"

She threw him a quick glance and pulled to a stop at a red light. "Have you got something against leaning?" she asked lightly. "You've got so much talent in that direction."

He grinned. "Hey, I'm a multitalented guy. I could flex if you want."

"Could you?" Laughter wanted to bubble up her throat, and that was curious. She hadn't really laughed in such a long, long time.

"Sure. And the jungle yell used to be a feature of mine in junior high. I could always bring it back."

She grinned. "I think I'll take a pass on that one. How are you at crushing beer cans on your forehead? There's always a lot of call for someone who can make a good clean crush."

He shook his head. "Never had a knack for it. Sorry. I guess I'll have to stick to leaning after all."

She smiled at him, wondering how he could be so dangerous and seem so gentle at the same time. Suddenly a picture from the past slid into her mind's eye and she saw it again as though it were yesterday, playing out in her head like a film. It was the annual school picnic at the beach. She could hear the old tapes playing in the background, feel the breezes that caressed her bare legs that day. She and a girl-friend were watching the volleyball game, sipping sodas and giggling over the players. Mack was one of them, and she could see him now, wearing nothing but the long, brightly colored shorts they used to wear then, his brown, rounded muscles gleaming in the sunlight, his hair a little too long, his face intent on the game. Watching him was beginning to make her uneasy for some reason she couldn't explain. She got up off the rock to go looking for Tom, and suddenly the ball landed right at her feet and Mack was careening into her, almost knocking her down. He stopped himself in time, grabbing her before she fell. She could still see the hard biceps of the arms that held her, feel the heat coming from his slick body.

"Are you okay?" he'd asked her.

She couldn't answer. Something inside was quivering, feeling weak and intoxicated at the same time. She couldn't look into his eyes. She remembered staring straight into the center of his muscular chest and nodding groggily. Without another word, he was gone, back to the game, and she was starting off on shaky legs, desperate to find Tom right away, as though finding good old safe, reliable Tom would some-how erase the terrifying feelings Mack seemed to conjure up in her.

"Then what is it?"

Mack was saying something, bringing her back to earth. She blinked at him. "What is what?"

"The substance of my job."

"Oh." It wasn't easy to pull her thoughts to the present. She'd forgotten how much she used to think about Mack, how big a part of her life he was, even though they hardly ever spoke to one another. She'd forgotten—but she was going to have to ignore it, push it out of her mind. She couldn't go around falling into dreams about him like this. And most of all, she could never, ever let him know that...

"Uh... We discussed this already. You're a deterrent." The light changed and she started up again, heading for the crossroads.

"I understand that," Mack said patiently. "What I'm not too clear on is the methods you want me to employ while I'm doing my deterring. I mean, what exactly do you want me to do, go around brandishing my firearm and yelling 'Make my day' at the local populace?"

"No, of course not." She frowned. It was hard telling him exactly what she wanted, because she wasn't sure of that herself. It was going to be whatever worked. For the most part, they were going to be playing this by ear. "For now, just kind of hover in the background looking malevolent."

His eyes turned cold. "So you can point at me and chortle with your friends?"

Aha. So that was what had brought this up. She stifled a grin. Funny how human he was turning out to be. "No. Did you think I was chortling?" She glanced at him and smiled. "No way. I was bragging."

"Bragging?" He frowned, looking almost petulant. "About what?"

She sighed. Either he was completely unaware of the figure he cut or he was fishing for compliments. Well, either way, she was full of her success in stirring Sue's juices, and she was ready to explain in full.

"Bragging about you." She grinned at him quickly. "I told Sue that you were mine." Her laugh was quick and happy. "My hired gun."

He groaned, sinking in the seat. "Oh, God. Not that."

"Believe me, she took one look and she was green with envy."

Unbelievably, he felt color creeping into his face. He couldn't remember the last time he'd been embarrassed. "Right."

She glanced at him. "No, I mean it. She really was." She pulled into a parking space in front of the little grocery store and turned off the engine, twisting in her seat to look at him and catching the tail end of a flush. Kimo Caine, blushing. It made her want to laugh, but she bit it back and teased him instead. "You're kind of a hunk you know. From a distance, anyway."

He groaned again, writhing in his seat, and this time she did laugh. "Oh, I love it. Now you're shy."

He sat up straighter and looked at her. He supposed it was only fair to warn her. "And you're dreaming," he drawled. "I may be embarrassed. But I'm not shy." His eyes met hers and held. "Not even a little bit," he added softly.

The smile faded from her lips and she looked away quickly. For some crazy reason her heart was beating a little too fast and a little too loudly. No, as tempting as it was to do so, she wasn't going to let him get to her. She frowned, trying to make herself concentrate.

"The point is, you don't have to *do* anything. Just be a presence. That's all. A very dangerous-looking presence."

If she'd still been watching, she would have seen the clouds gathering in his dark eyes as he thought that over. In other words, she wanted him to be the bad boy. No problem. He'd been the bad guy all his life. Did she realize what she was asking him to do here? It didn't seem so. He didn't think it had occurred to her. Maybe he was going to have to clue her in.

Or maybe she didn't care. Why should she care? After all, she just wanted a job done. His feelings were irrelevant. And she had every right to think so. He was just a hired gun, doing a job. And he'd better not forget it.

"Think it would help if we got a black patch to put across one eye?" he asked, only partly in jest. "Maybe I should grow one of those scruffy beards."

She gave him a sideways look. "It looks like you've already started doing that."

His hand went to his chin and he sighed. "Sorry about that. I guess I forgot."

Turning, she looked him over. He really did look great—just hard enough to be on the verge of scary, just cool enough to be capable of anything. The only thing that tended to work against the image was his naturally handsome face, only slightly marred by the ugly scar that slashed across it. And the unshaven shadow tended to obscure that. "It's okay. It gives you a good rough-and-ready look."

"Rough-and-ready, huh?" Whatever. He wanted to help her, and if that was what she needed... "I guess that is what we're going for here." He shrugged, trying to be helpful. "I could slash my jeans. Tie a bandanna around my head. Wear an ammunition belt strung across my chest, like a bandito."

She smiled, relieved that he was keeping it light. "That would be a lovely touch. Not too stylish, though."

He raised one eyebrow and held her gaze again. "I've never been known for my style."

Somehow there was more in what he had just said than the words would lead one to believe. It was time for her to turn away, time to get this show on the road. But instead, she found herself falling in with his tone, saying, "No? Just what are you known for?" She felt like a woman in a trance, mesmerized by his dark eyes, soothed by his low voice.

"Action," he answered softly, his head tilting back. "Performance. Coming through in the clutch."

She realized they weren't talking about what they'd started talking about, and a flush began to spread across her face. This banter felt all too enticing with him. She was going to have to watch her step or she would find herself in deep trouble.

"Well, the only performance I'm interested in is how you perform in helping me keep terrorists off my ranch," she said firmly, turning away and reaching for the door handle.

"Of course," he said smoothly, following her, his mouth only slightly twisted in a smile. "What else?"

But he knew what else as well as she did, and he also knew that he had to stop teasing her. And she had probably better stop teasing him, too. Teasing was only going to get them both in trouble.

It was hard to stop, though. She was cuter than heck when she got embarrassed. There was something about her that still pulled at him as it always had. And teasing just came naturally to him when he was around attractive women.

He got out of the car and looked around. He remembered this place. It had changed, but it was still so much the same. How could it still be so much the same after all these years? Probably because this little bare excuse for a town was hidden back in the shelter of the blue-green mountains, away from the tourist traps along the coast, away from the big hotels on the other side of the island. It looked like any Cowtown Crossroads, USA. Almost. If you looked too closely, you saw the palm trees in the background, smelled the ginger and the plumeria in the air. But that was just what he liked about it. In his dreams this was what heaven looked like.

It was really too warm for his leather jacket, but if he took it off, the bulge where he wore his weapon would be apparent. Maybe that was what Taylor wanted, but it wasn't what he wanted. He'd never been one to look for trouble. He did seem to attract it, and he'd learned to deal with it when it appeared, but it wasn't something he enjoyed.

So what are you doing here? a part of his mind jeered at him. What the hell are you doing, getting into the middle of a neighborhood dispute? The most dangerous thing around, after a marital squabble, was a dispute between neighbors. They were just as full of emotion and unresolved grudges, and just as uncontrollable. What was he doing in the middle?

I'm not in the middle, he silently said to his conscience. I'm on Taylor's side.

And just what did being on Taylor's side mean?

He had started to follow her, heading for the entrance to the store, when he was accosted by a slim figure coming the other way. The woman nodded at Taylor as she passed her, but her attention was all on Mack.

"Hey, Mack," said Lani Tanaka, turning her baseball cap backward on her head before stopping in front of him.

He grinned, stopping to stand with his legs set apart and his head back. "Hey, Lani."

"How's it going?" Lani asked, glancing at Taylor, who was lingering, then slipping on a huge pair of dark glasses.

"Just fine. How about you?"

She shrugged in answer. "So you got there okay?"

"Yup. Thanks for the ride."

"No problem." She slid her hands into the back pockets of her jeans and tilted her face up toward his. "Listen, there've been people all over that plane of yours all afternoon."

Mack's head went back and a wariness entered his gaze. When it came to his PBY, he was very protective. "That's fine, as long as they look and don't touch."

"Oh, they're lookin' all right. And asking how much you want for it."

He frowned. "Who's asking that?"

"A local bigwig named Bart Carlson." She jerked her thumb toward where Taylor stood, listening. "She knows him."

"Bart Carlson?" Taylor and Mack repeated in unison, and Taylor stepped closer.

"Yup. He collects vintage aircraft. He's got a hanger on his own land, and a small airstrip. He was all over your PBY with his tongue hanging out."

Mack and Taylor exchanged glances. "That's interesting," he muttered.

"Yeah." Lani moved restlessly, starting to edge toward her vehicle. "You could probably get him to cough up major money if you wanted to sell."

Mack shook his head, dismissing that out of hand. "Selling that plane would be like selling my firstborn child. No amount of money would ever be enough."

Lani shrugged and turned to go. "I'll tell him that if he shows up this afternoon. See you 'round."

"Lani," Taylor called after her. "Say hi to your mom, okay?"

Lani waved without looking back. "Will do."

Taylor stepped up and stood beside Mack as they watched her depart on her little motorcycle.

"So where did you meet Lani?" Taylor asked quietly.

"She gave me a ride in from the airport."

"Ah." Taylor smiled. "You know who her mom is, don't you?"

Mack looked at her. "No. Who?"

She tried to suppress a bubble of laughter that turned into a hiccup. "Sherry Tanaka. Used to be Sherry Hall."

"Sherry Hall?" he repeated doubtfully. Then memories surfaced. "*Sherry Hall.* Wasn't she the one who was always leading protest marches through the quad?"

"The original feminist. The first one in our class to burn her bra. Remember when she sat on the principal's car and wouldn't get off until he promised to let girls try out for the football team?"

"Yeah." He laughed. "And then she was the only one who showed up for workout. Boy, did she look weird in those shoulder pads."

Taylor nodded. "She married Buddy Tanaka and they have six kids now."

"Funny." His gaze met hers and they both laughed.

The laugh went on a little too long. Somehow it was warming to share something like that with her. He didn't want the feeling to stop. She was the one who looked away first.

"So what is this plane of yours that Bart is interested in?"

"A reconditioned PBY. A relic from World War II that I restored. I flew it in from the mainland."

She bit her lip and frowned. "Strange that Bart should zero in on that without even knowing about our connection."

Connection. He liked that word.

"Very strange," he agreed.

She thought about it a moment more, her brow furrowed. Then she shook it off and turned. "Well, let's get going," she said briskly. "We don't have much time left, and I want to make sure Bart hears about you by nightfall."

The country store was a simple affair, not much bigger than a convenience store, but every inch was stocked to the rafters and beyond with every item imaginable. Along one side there was a small lunch counter that specialized in hot steaming bowls of saimin noodles and little sticks of barbecued meat. Along another were things made by locals and sold on consignment, everything from handmade quilts to home-canned mangoes. The smells were an exotic mixture of Occident and Orient, and Mack took a deep breath. Though he didn't think he'd ever been in this particular store before, he'd been in plenty like it. It smelled like home. It had been a long, long time.

"Hi, Abby." Taylor waved at the older woman as they entered the store. "I want you to meet somebody."

Abby Kuramada looked up with a smile that quickly faded as she caught sight of Mack. Her eyes were riveted to him as though she was afraid he was about to start stuffing things into the pockets of that leather jacket.

"It's okay, Abby," Taylor said quickly. "He's with me."

"With you?" Abby frowned.

"He's my..." Taylor looked at Mack quickly and made an adjustment. "He's my bodyguard," she said decisively. "Abby, this is Mack Caine. I've hired him for protection."

"Oh, a bodyguard?" The woman looked perplexed, her dark-eyed gaze traveling from Taylor to Mack and back again. "What do you need a bodyguard for? Someone trying to hurt you, Taylor?"

Taylor looked at Abby and decided not to get too explicit. She didn't want to frighten her old friend. "Well, somebody might be. I decided I needed protection, so I hired him."

Abby's stern face still showed disapproval. Slowly, she leaned closer to Taylor, her gaze still on Mack. "Yeah?" she whispered. "Well, tell me this, Taylor, my dear. Who's going to protect *you* from your protector?"

"That woman doesn't like me," Mack noted as they got in the car and prepared to go just a few buildings down to the filling station.

"Oh, she likes you just fine. She's just worried about me," Taylor told him comfortably. "She and my mother were good friends, and she always feels sort of responsible for me."

Mack turned and looked at her. "Your mother?"

"She died ten years ago. Cancer."

He remembered her, a thin, nervous woman who smoked too much. "I'm sorry."

Taylor felt a lump rise in her throat and that startled her. She didn't usually do that anymore. Not like at first. "I'm sorry, too," she managed to say with her voice breaking only slightly. "I sure do miss her."

He wanted to say something, reach for her, but he didn't want to overstep his place in this relationship, and they were already pulling up to the pump at the filling station.

Taylor hopped out. "Will you fill her up?" she asked Mack. "I'll go into the office and tell Danny all about you."

"You'd be able to tell him more," Mack muttered to himself as he got out of the car and went to the pump, "if you really knew me, Taylor."

But that wasn't the point, and he understood that. And Taylor was already in the glass-enclosed office, talking to a lanky redheaded kid who was staring out at him, slack jawed.

"Just look tough," he reminded himself, squaring his shoulders and setting his head at an arrogant tilt. "That's how you earn your keep these days. Nice work, if you can get it."

Taylor was working, too, working hard at putting across an image Danny wouldn't be able to erase from his mind, no matter how hard he tried. She knew Bart came in here all the time, knew he chatted with Danny on a daily basis. And she wanted to be sure Danny would have an earful for the man the next time he stopped in.

"Danny, just between you and me, I hired Mack to protect my ranch," she was saying, leaning on the little counter that held the gum and candy and other items Danny sold on the side. "Someone's been trying to terrorize me. So I hired myself someone who has a lot of experience in this sort of thing."

Danny hadn't taken his eyes off Mack yet. "Like in the Westerns."

"Exactly." She smiled. This was easy as pie. "He's real experienced in controlling situations, if you know what I mean."

"Huh?" He glanced at her, then went right back to staring at Mack. "Oh. Right."

"You see, that's what I brought him in for. To control my situation." She leaned closer to the boy. "Just as you said, it's like the Western movies. You've got the big cattle baron who controls the whole town. And then you've got your little family farm that the cattle baron is trying to squeeze out. And, of course, your innocent little town folk. All the little people in the town and on the farm get together and hire a gunslinger to come in and stand up for them against the evil cattle baron. That's what I did."

"Huh?" He was still staring out, watching Mack finish off the pumping and put the nozzle back.

"I hired myself a gunslinger."

He turned and stared at her. "You're kidding."

She smiled, feeling smug again. "His name's Mack Caine. His great-grandfather was a pirate."

Danny's eyes got even wider. "Far out."

"Yes, Danny. This is very far out. And he is very tough. He's done mercenary work for some big people down in South America." She didn't suppose that was really true, but it did get the point across and sounded good.

Danny swallowed hard and looked out at Mack again. "A real mercenary?"

"Yup. He's been involved in all those little wars and things down there. And now he's here."

"Oh, wow. I wish you all the luck in the world, Ms. Taggert. But be careful. He looks..."

Mack was walking toward the office. She could tell by the way Danny was looking at Mack that he expected bullets to drop from his jacket when he walked and blood to ooze from between his teeth when he smiled. He was blinking rapidly and even backed up as far as he could as Mack approached.

"Hey," Mack said, nodding at him. He flexed his shoulders and frowned, just lookin' tough. "How you doin'?"

"O-okay." Danny gaped at him.

Mack returned the look for a moment, then threw a quizzical glance at Taylor and began to look at the things for sale under the counter.

"Can I get something for you?" Danny asked eagerly. "I mean, it would be on the house. If... if you need something special... I mean, I know some people who could .."

He glanced at Taylor and she knew he was talking about booze or ammunition or something almost illegal like that. He was dying to get in good with the gunslinger.

Mack started to shake his head, and then he stopped. "You know, I do need something," he said, frowning as he looked over the stock again. "You got any hand lotion in there anywhere?" He pointed at a tube he saw behind the counter. "Is that the kind that smells like roses? I like that stuff."

"Roses?" Danny turned to look at Taylor, at a loss. This hardly fit his image of a gunslinger. "Hand lotion?" he asked her pitiably, looking like a boy who'd just been told the tooth fairy had gone on strike.

She rolled her eyes. Turning on her heel, she grabbed Mack by the arm and pulled him into the sunshine.

"You ruined everything," she stormed at him. "I had him believing you were a killer on the road, and you walk in and ask for hand lotion."

He shook his head, unable to see what the problem was. "I asked for hand lotion because I wanted hand lotion."

"Oh!" She glared at him in frustration. "What did you want hand lotion for?"

He held out his hands. "Because my skin is dry. If you think about it, there's a logical connection here."

She knew he had a point, but she wasn't about to concede it. "I've got some in the car," she said grumpily. "Come on."

He fell into step beside her. "So you think he's decided I'm a poofter and no threat to anyone?"

"No." She sighed, then met his gaze and laughed softly. "Of course not. I guess I might be getting a little carried away with this."

He reached in front of her and opened her car door, nodding. "Just a little," he agreed.

Before getting in, she put a hand on his arm. "Thanks, Mack," she said sincerely. "You've been great."

He looked at her slender fingers against his arm, then raised his gaze to meet hers. It was the old Taylor he saw there, so close, so accessible. He could take her into his arms right now and she couldn't stop him. He could finally taste her mouth, finally go beyond dreams.

Everything he was thinking must have been showing in his face, because she drew away from him as though he'd suddenly changed into the wolf man right in front of her. Avoiding his eyes, she began to babble senselessly about the encounter with Danny, slipping into the car and starting it without waiting for him to get in.

But he did get in, and they drove off. She continued to complain for another few moments as they turned down the highway, but he didn't pay any attention. He was busy taking in the scenery, connecting with his past and wondering why nothing ever really changed.

He'd been gone for so many years, seen so much, lived a completely different life, and yet this was home. He could feel it, taste it, smell it. No matter where he roamed or how long he was gone, this would always be home. Nothing could ever change that.

And it seemed that nothing would ever change his yearning for Taylor. The only problem was, he could never let her know.

It was just before five when they pulled into Sue's driveway.

"They're playing out back," Taylor noted. "I'll just run out and get Ryan."

She slipped out of the car, almost relieved to get away from Mack for a moment or two. It was amazing how variable things were with him. One moment they were light-hearted together, almost on the verge of having fun, the next that dark and dangerous mood seemed to seize him. She wasn't sure what it meant, but she was pretty sure she was going to have to deal with it sooner or later.

In just hours, he'd made himself a part of her life. How had that happened? He was just supposed to be an employee. If he hadn't turned out to be someone from her past, it wouldn't have happened. But it had turned out to be Kimo Caine, a part of her past forever shrouded in the thrill of awakening sexuality and the mystery dangerous boys held for good girls like her. And somehow, that had made him important, then and now.

"It won't last long," she whispered as she made her way quickly to the side of the house. "As we get to know each other, the exotic aspects will fade and we'll deal with each other just like any other old friends."

Maybe. She had to keep hoping.

She'd come even with the corner of the house when the long, low sports car came shooting in, cutting around where her car was parked in the driveway and jerking to a screeching halt just inches away from her.

"Taylor." Bart Carlson unfolded his tall body from behind the wheel and strode toward where she was backing away. "Wait a moment. I must talk to you."

"I don't want to talk to you, Bart," she said angrily. "Just leave me alone."

She tried to turn and slip away from him, but his hand shot out and captured her arm, the fingers biting into her flesh.

"Now you just hold it right there, young lady," he said harshly. "You're going to listen to me if I have to drag you back to my place and—"

That was as far as he got before Mack arrived. He came up quickly but he didn't seem to make a sound. He was just suddenly there. Bart turned, startled, and stared at him.

"Hello, Carlson," Mack said, his voice like broken glass on porcelain. "I wouldn't do that if I were you."

Involuntarily, Bart's hand opened and fell away from Taylor's arm. Mack nodded his approval. Bart looked annoyed that he'd done it.

"You keep leaving your fingerprints on women," Mack drawled, his eyes a dangerous shade of jet, "and pretty soon they're going to have to lock you away."

Bart glared at him, flexing his hands as though he were considering using them to leave some fingerprints on Mack's neck. He was a tall man, in his forties, with brown, receding hair and a look that left no doubt as to his superiority to everyone else. He peered at Mack speculatively and nodded as though he had realized something important.

"You ought to know a lot about that," he said in a nasty tone. "Didn't I have to swear out a warrant for your arrest once upon a time?" His eyes narrowed. "Aren't you Kimo Caine? Didn't you break into my house a few years ago?"

Finally, somebody recognized him off the bat, and it had to be Bart Carlson. Mack couldn't help but smile at the irony. It wasn't, however, a gratifying reunion. The man's accusation cut like a searing knife through Mack's chest. The past just wasn't that far away, was it?

"You've got a good memory, Carlson," he said, maintaining the lazy smile with difficulty. "If your memory is so good, surely you remember the second half of that story. It wasn't long before those charges were dropped."

Bart's sneer was finally back, and he used it to good effect. "That's the problem with the law today. Too many criminals get off on technicalities."

Mack took the insult and returned, "And others just hide behind respectable covers, pretending to be what they aren't."

Bart continued to sneer, but he didn't seem to have a response to that. "What are you doing back in town?" he asked instead.

Mack shrugged. "I've got a job."

"What kind of job?" he said, with the air of someone who could do something to change that.

Mack glanced at Taylor. She hadn't said a word since he'd arrived, but she was the one who wanted Bart to know about him, so he figured he might as well plow on ahead. "I'm working for Taylor. She needed someone to protect her and her property, and I volunteered."

Bart turned and glared at Taylor. "What kind of nonsense is this?" he demanded.

Taylor's eyes were clear and angry. "I've hired myself a gunslinger of my own, Bart." She glared at him defiantly.

He began to look like a man besieged, a man who truly didn't know why everyone seemed to be ganging up on him. "Taylor, what did you go and hire this punk for? If you need protection, you know I'm ready to help you anytime. I could send over one of my men—"

Taylor's laugh was short and lacking any noticeable humor. "No dice, Bart. Strange things have been happening on my place lately. Someone seems to be trying to run me off the land."

He shook his head and stepped toward her, his hands out. "I told you I'd take care of that if you'd just—"

She took a step backward and glanced over to make sure Mack was ready to help if she needed him. "I need an independent source of protection, Bart. I can't prove you're behind my miseries, but you certainly are one of the main suspects."

"What? Me?" The man seemed genuinely at a loss for words. "Taylor. No, now how can you say such a thing?"

Ryan appeared from the backyard, looking at the three of them curiously as he skipped on past, going for his mother's car.

"Hey, little fella," Bart called out, trying for hearty and coming out very strained. "Where you going so fast?"

Ryan stopped and looked at Bart. "Hi," he said uncertainly. He could tell the adults were arguing and he didn't want to get in the middle.

"Go on to the car, Ryan," Taylor said. She took Mack by the arm. "Let's go," she said, throwing a piercing glare at Bart. "It's time to get on home."

They turned, walked to the car and got in. Bart didn't move. He watched them go like a man who couldn't understand where he'd gone wrong. Taylor backed the car out of the drive and took off down the highway.

"So," she said brightly. "That was Bart. What do you think?"

Mack grinned. "I think he's madder than hell."

She looked at him. "I think you're right." And they both laughed.

They didn't talk more about it on the way home. Taylor waited until Ryan was out of the car and running inside to catch his favorite TV show before she went back to the subject.

"You looked real mean," she told Mack happily as they slowly vacated the car.

He glanced at her, wondering when that had become a compliment. "I did?"

"Yeah." She nodded and smiled. "You looked real bad. And that was good."

The smile faded from his eyes and he leaned against the car, looking at her through his lashes. "It was good to look bad?"

"Sure. We want to scare him." She sighed happily, then recalled something that sobered her. "I didn't know he would remember you that way."

Mack nodded and looked toward the mountains. "Oh, Bart and I go way back. He had me arrested a couple of times."

Arrested. What a strange concept that was to her. She shivered, but she didn't turn away.

"Why didn't you tell me?"

Why didn't he tell her? Was she kidding? His gaze flickered over her again. "There was nothing to tell. It was all a very long time ago."

She hesitated, then asked softly, "Were you guilty?"

He stiffened. She couldn't have said anything more calculated to cut him. When he met her gaze, his eyes were hard and his tone bitter. "Wasn't I always?" he said harshly.

And with that, he drew himself up and strode into the house, leaving her behind.

Five

Dinner was a strained affair with Taylor not sure what had turned Mack dark and moody again. But in some ways it was a relief. His silence gave her time to assimilate all that had happened since he'd wandered into her yard earlier that afternoon. She felt as though she'd gone through a week's worth of emotions since then. It was good to have space to put different parts of the experience into proportion.

Bottom line, she'd hired a dangerous man to protect her from an even more dangerous situation. That was very much like buying a gun to protect oneself from robbers. The remedy itself was almost as dangerous as the disease. Just as one had to handle a gun very carefully, she would have to handle Mack with kid gloves. And she would also have to remind him often and firmly that she was the boss.

"I need to meet with you right after I finish the dishes," she told him as he helped her clear the table. "We have some things to discuss."

He hesitated. Jill had hated it when he did things to help her in the kitchen. She always claimed he made more work than he helped with. But Taylor wasn't Jill. Maybe she wanted a hand.

"I can dry," he offered.

She looked at him in surprise, inordinately pleased at such a simple offer. But then she turned away, not letting him see. "No, thanks," she said quickly. "I've got some things to think over and I can do that better alone. Besides," she added with a smile as he moved to go. "I've got a dishwasher. No drying needed."

That didn't mollify him. He felt oddly out of place. Leaving the kitchen, he wandered through the house, then followed the sound of cartoons to the back room where Ryan was watching television.

The door was open to the denlike room. He went in and leaned on the wall. "What are you watching?" he asked.

Ryan looked up grudgingly. He hadn't said anything all through dinner, except "Please pass the butter." And he obviously wasn't about to become chatty now.

"The Masked Mallard," he muttered.

"Ah, the terror that flaps in the night." Mack grinned in recognition. "So you like the punster, do you?"

Ryan's scowl looked a mite less ferocious. "Do you watch him?" he asked, seemingly astonished.

Mack nodded. "I've been known to indulge upon occasion."

The boy's eyes narrowed suspiciously. "What's your favorite one?"

"Hmm." Mac stroked his chin. This was obviously a test. "I kind of favor the one where the pods take over and the cows are not as they seem. How about you?"

A light sprang into the boy's eyes. He couldn't resist. "I like the one where Taurus Bulba comes back to life."

"That's a good one, too."

Ryan stared at him a moment more, then turned his attention to the screen, but he didn't protest when Mack slid down to sit on the couch beside him, and pretty soon they were both chuckling over the silly jokes.

It was strange how much the kid looked like his father. Mack wondered if he was going to be able to get beyond that and actually like him. Only time would tell.

Taylor appeared in the doorway just as the show was winding down and motioned to him. He rose, winked at the boy and followed her into the dining room. This time she sat at the dining room table, and he sat across from her. She had her boss-lady face on. He felt like a kid being called in to the principal's office.

She pulled open the infamous ledger and looked over a list before she raised her eyes and met his. "Okay, here's the deal," she said crisply. "I told you that the bunkhouse burned down. That means you're going to have to stay in the house."

He nodded, not seeing the problem yet. He'd assumed as much. He knew her other hands all lived nearby, except for Josi, who had his own little hut down the hill, a place he'd kept for himself for the past fifty years. There was no place else. Of course he was staying here.

"That means we're going to be sharing a house together. So we have to set the ground rules."

"Ground rules?" He felt mildly insulted. So this was what she'd been thinking over all evening. Sitting back in the chair, he leveled an icy glare at her. "What do you think I am, Taylor? Some sort of animal who needs to be caged at night?"

She had the grace to flush a bit, but that didn't keep her from sticking to her guns. "I don't know what you are, Mack. When you come right down to it, I don't know you at all. And I really don't think I *want* to know you. But I want you to know me, what I want, how it's going to be. Otherwise this won't work at all.''

He felt anger beginning to swell in his gut and he had to hold it back. After all, she had every right to say these things. He knew she was only trying to keep control of the situation. But he also knew she wouldn't feel this need to establish her authority if it wasn't for the way she looked at him. He was still a bad guy in her book. That stung. But he was going to have to learn to live with it.

There was really no point taking offense. The only way he could come out of this without going crazy was to see the humor in it. Humor. There had to be something funny.

''Okay, shoot,'' he said calmly, looking her over. ''How's it going to be?''

She hesitated, licking her dry lips. She'd started out strong, but evidently it was going to be harder for her to talk about this than she'd first thought. Her gaze wavered for just a moment, but then she hardened it again. She had to maintain a certain amount of attitude or she would lose it all.

''I hired you to do a job for me, a job that is going to require you to be here twenty-four hours a day. You're going to eat here, and I'll provide you with food. And you're going to sleep here, and I'll give you a place to do that.'' She sat up a little taller and folded her hands in front of her. ''But that's it. We're not going to be friends. And we're definitely not going to be . . . more than friends.''

''More than friends?'' He gazed at her with complete innocence. It looked as though there might be some humor to be found in the situation after all. ''Why, Taylor, whatever do you mean?''

Now she really was blushing, damn it all. ''You know what I mean,'' she said tightly, avoiding his gaze.

He leaned forward across the table. ''You mean no seducing, right?'' he said in a loud stage whisper. ''No kisses in the night, no lingering looks, no casual touches that stir fires...."

Her blue eyes flashed and glared at him. "That's exactly what I mean, and don't laugh at me."

Straightening, he sobered. "I'm not laughing, Taylor. Believe me, you thinking I might attack you in the night is no laughing matter to me."

"I didn't say that." She looked distressed, shaking her head. "I... Look, you've got to understand something. I've been a widow for almost a year, and I've heard it all. Every man I meet seems to think I'm pining for something only he can give me. And every one of them thinks he can provide what I've been missing." Her spirit of anger was returning as she went through the litany. "Well, guess what. I'm not missing a thing. My husband was all the man I'll ever need. You can do me a favor by remembering that. As far as I'm concerned, I'm still married to him."

It seemed odd that good old Tom could still bring forth this kind of declaration of commitment. Tom had been a winner in his day. In high school, he'd won just about everything he'd touched. They'd crowned him the fair-haired child, the champion of all he surveyed. But there had been a streak of weakness in him, a streak that Mack probably knew more about than most. She'd been married to him. Hadn't she ever seen it? If so, she'd found a way to deny it. But then, maybe it was just as well.

And maybe he was just jealous. Jealous of a dead man.

Mack sighed and rose from the table. "Don't worry, Taylor. I'm not going to force myself on you. Now if you'll just show me where my room is, I'm still running on mainland time and I figure I haven't had any sleep for about thirty hours."

Taylor stayed where she was and watched him, suddenly feeling weary. "There's a room at the end of the hall, right next to the den where you were watching TV with Ryan.

There's a bathroom right across the hall. I set out towels for you and gave you fresh sheets.''

He looked at her, his eyes dark and hooded, and for some reason her heart was suddenly pounding like crazy in her chest. He stood there a beat too long, and she waited, almost holding her breath. But the moment passed, and he seemed to shrug. "Good night" was all he said, and then he was walking down the hall, walking away from her, and she breathed a long, low sigh of relief.

She was playing with fire here, and she knew it. She tried not to watch him saunter down the hall, but she couldn't pull her gaze away. He moved like a beautiful animal, all strength and grace, in a way that would make her ache inside if she let it. But she wasn't going to let it. She wasn't going to allow her libido to come to life again. It had been dormant for a long, long time, and she didn't see any benefit in letting it come back. It would only make it that much harder to let him go when this was over. She knew that. She wasn't an idiot. She had a son to protect. She had goals and she meant to achieve them. There would be no time for romance.

It really was a good thing she was immune to that sort of thing now. Because she'd meant every word she'd said. She would never fall in love again. There was no percentage in it. Love was hard work. And she was tired.

It was after midnight when she awoke. She was wide-awake immediately and she lay very still and tried to listen over the beating of her heart, listen for what had awakened her. She'd heard footsteps. Someone was right outside her window.

She moved slowly, softly, trying to glide, trying not to make a sound, until she'd made her way to the window. Heart pounding in her throat, she pulled the curtain aside enough to see out. A dark form was just disappearing around the corner of the house.

She never doubted it was Bart or one of his henchmen. If the threat of having a bodyguard on the property wasn't enough to deter them, she was going to have to take more direct action. Moving quickly and as quietly as she could, she slipped through the house and unlocked the closet door where she kept her shotgun. Weapon in hand, she went through the kitchen and stole onto the back porch, moving like a shadow.

The air was cool on her skin, and the light breeze flattened her long white nightgown to her legs, hindering her movements. She hardly noticed. She could just make out the outline of a form walking toward the stables, and she followed, walking on the side of the gravel walk so that her footsteps would be muffled by the grass. She lost sight of him as the path curved, and when she came to the bend, suddenly there he was, turned to look over the valley.

She didn't stop to think. She had to react. There was no time for anything else. Swinging the shotgun into place, she yelled, "Stop or I'll shoot."

The figure turned and looked at her, but didn't seem unduly perturbed.

"Not again," it said in complete disgust.

Taylor raised her head and stared at the shadow. Belatedly, she realized it looked a lot like Mack. Sounded a bit like him, too. "Oh," she said, disappointed. "It's you."

"It's me. Don't shoot. Terminating your employees this way is considered bad form in some circles. I realize that cramps your style, but that's the breaks, kid."

"I'm not going to shoot you." She lowered the shotgun and caught her breath, waiting for the adrenaline to calm down. Then she went on the offensive. "What are you doing out here? I thought you were Bart or one of his men."

He shrugged. "I woke up. The time zones are all messed up in my head. It'll take a while to settle that down. But I thought, as long as I was awake, I'd come on out and look around, just make sure everything was battened down."

He stared at her, admiring the flimsy white nightgown. She looked like an angel in the darkness. Moonlight spilled silver on her hair, but he could barely make out her eyes. He wished he could see into them and read her thoughts.

Then something occurred to him and he frowned. "But Taylor, why did you come out after me on your own? Why didn't you go in and try to wake me up?"

She looked at him quickly and drew her arms in close, not too sure of the answer to that herself. "I ... I don't know. I'm just so used to taking care of things by myself...."

He turned away. He didn't buy it. She still didn't trust him. She'd hired him all the way from Los Angeles, expecting to trust him, and then when she'd found out who he was, her trust had evaporated. What was he going to have to do to erase her doubts? But maybe that wasn't even possible. After all, he'd been saddled with this reputation for the past twenty years. Maybe he was branded for life. Maybe it never changed.

"We're going to have to work out some sort of signal so that I don't end up getting shot," he said, moving restlessly and looking over the valley again. "You're just a little too trigger-happy for my taste, boss lady."

She had to bite her tongue to keep from telling him not to call her that. She hated it. But at the same time, she knew it was good. It kept the roles straight. She was the boss. He was the employee.

So what was she doing out here waltzing around half dressed in front of the help? It was time to head for the house, time to cut this little encounter short, and she knew it. But there was something about the way his shoulders seemed to droop, something about the resigned, world-weary tone of his voice, that wouldn't let her go.

She hesitated, then made up her mind. Ordinarily she wouldn't have been caught dead anywhere near him in this sheer nightgown, but the night was dark and she felt protected by that. She stepped closer, standing beside him, looking out at what he was gazing at—the dark and twisted shadows of the night.

"Does it feel good to be back?" she asked him softly. "Are you planning to stay?"

"Planning?" He stuck his hands into the back pockets of his jeans and looked at her. His voice was rough with something she couldn't identify. "Plans are for people like you, Taylor. People with families and roots. I don't plan anything. I just wait to see what's going to happen."

"But you had a family once. You were married." She waited, but he didn't volunteer anything, so she went on. "Did you have any children?"

The question sliced into him with unexpected pain, and he saw Jill again, saw her as she'd looked the last time he'd seen her, six months pregnant. His wife, who had always refused his desire for children, had always said his job was much too dangerous for them to bring children into the world, was six months pregnant with another man's baby.

"No," he said gruffly. "No children."

She could feel his pain, though she didn't know exactly what had caused it. The agony radiated from him, and suddenly she couldn't bear it. Reaching out, she put her hand on his arm.

"What is it, Mack?" she asked softly. "Can I do anything to..."

When he turned to look at her, his eyes were burning. She could have drawn away then, but she didn't, and he moved toward her, his hand raking into her hair, cupping the back of her head, and she knew in another second he was going to kiss her.

It was too much. "No!" she cried out, jerking herself away. "Don't touch me."

"No touching?" he repeated coolly, snatching his hand back as though she'd slapped him. This was crazy. He wasn't totally naive. He'd felt her compassion, felt her warmth. She'd wanted him to kiss her. Why couldn't she admit it to herself? "What's the matter, Taylor?" His eyes narrowed. "Who hurt you?"

"Nobody hurt me." Both her hands went to her throat and she took a very deep breath. "I . . . I just have to stand alone, don't you see? I can't let you touch me. I can't let anyone touch me."

No, this didn't compute. There was more here than she was admitting. "Did Tom—"

"No," she said vehemently. The last thing in the world she wanted to do was give anyone the impression that Tom had abused her in any way. "No, I swear to you, Tom never hurt me. You've been watching too many afternoon talk shows."

It wasn't Tom. Not directly. How could she explain to Mack that he was just too dangerous? She couldn't risk letting him get that close. Without saying another word, she turned and began to walk toward the house.

He fell into step beside her. "Tell me, Taylor," he said quietly. "What was life with Tom like?"

"Tom?" Why was her mouth so dry? "He was my husband."

"You made it quite clear earlier that you loved him very deeply."

"Yes."

"That he was everything he could have been to you."

"Exactly."

His dark eyes bored into her in the shadows. "Then why do I get the feeling that there's more to the story?"

She reacted quickly, defensively. "If there is more to the story, it's not there for you."

"So you're going to keep it bottled up inside. Take it to your grave."

She sighed with impatience. "Take what to my grave? There's nothing to take."

"Then why are you so sensitive?"

She stopped and stood on the path, her arms thrown up in exasperation. "Listen. Tom and I went together all through high school. We went to Honolulu together and stayed close all through college. We came back here and got married and had a child, and while he was alive, we had a very happy life together. End of story."

End of any story she would ever tell him. Or anyone. Life with Tom had not been a bowl of cherries, but so what? Whose life was perfect, anyway?

Mack walked to the edge of the path and looked out over the meadow and up toward where the purple mountains made a jagged edge against a velvet blue sky. He knew she wasn't telling him everything. And he'd known Tom. He knew what a bastard the jerk could be. "How did he die?"

She felt stiff, tight, fragile, as though she were made of glass. "It was a hunting accident. He and a group of friends liked to hunt wild boar over on the other side of the island." She steadied herself. This was no good. She didn't have to defend her marriage to Tom. After all, Mack had known him. Putting her hands on her hips, she glared at him. "Why do you insist on doing this? I had a happy marriage, Mack. Don't think otherwise. I loved Tom very, very much. He was a wonderful father. And I don't want Ryan ever to think any differently."

She closed her eyes and turned around. She shouldn't have said that last sentence. It gave a little too much away.

The truth was, it was for Ryan she was denying there had ever been anything wrong in her marriage. Ryan must never know the truth about his father. Ryan must always think only good things about his dad. That was part of the legacy she was determined to give him.

Mack watched her, wanting badly to take her in his arms and soothe away the torture he could feel her going through. She could deny it all she wanted, but she needed love. She needed warmth and affection, just like anybody else. Why couldn't she accept it from him? Was it because of the way she thought of him? Did she think he wasn't good enough?

But what the hell—he'd told himself he wasn't going to get caught up in that sort of thing, anyway. Hadn't he? It was for the best. Besides, reality never turned out as good as dreams.

"We'd better go in."

"In a minute. I want to breathe it all in. Suck it into my lungs and take it into the center of my soul. You know what I mean? I need this. It's like food to me."

She hesitated, knowing she should go. Instead, she stepped close to him, as though she was tempting fate—and tempting herself. "Did you miss Hawaii all these years on the mainland?" she asked softly.

He nodded. "I didn't realize how much," he said. And that was true. For years he'd thought he was happy with his work and his marriage. If only Jill had told him sooner how terribly unhappy she was, he might have done something. He might have brought her here, home, and he might have saved his marriage.

But what if he'd brought Jill here and then he'd run into Taylor...?

What the hell was he thinking of? That would never have happened. And if he still had Jill, he wouldn't look twice at Taylor. She was a high school crush, that was all. Jill was his wife.

Was. That was the operative word. Jill was his wife no longer. She was now married to Randy Trout, his old partner. His wife and his best friend. How corny could you get? His life was the sort of sloppy mess they wrote country and western songs about.

"Do you really remember me from the old days, Taylor?" he asked softly. "Do you remember trig class?"

She hesitated. She didn't want to do anything that would draw them closer together. And yet, she couldn't resist.

"I remember that," she admitted.

"And the way I was always getting into trouble." His voice took on a sarcastic tone. "Surely you remember that."

Of course she remembered. It was all true, wasn't it? "I do. I remember when you were suspended for fighting with that boy in the quad."

He nodded. "Jeremy Papp. That one I deserved."

"And I remember when you..." Did she really want to get into this? But she had to. "When you got Amy Fosselburg pregnant."

He stiffened beside her and turned, glaring. "I did not get Amy Fosselburg pregnant." A rage fueled by all the old lies filled him.

Taylor shook her head, feeling defensive. What was he going to do, rewrite history? "She said it was you."

He had to take a deep breath to keep his temper in check. "I slept with Amy Fosselburg one time and one time only. She came on to me when I was drunk. Otherwise I never would have touched her."

There was something important happening here. She could feel it. This had to be confronted, had to be taken care of. Ordinarily, she would never accuse anyone of anything like this, even if she was sure it was true. But this was a different case. This went to the heart of how they were going to be dealing with one another from now on. They both sensed it.

"She didn't tell the story quite that way," Taylor said evenly.

He grunted. "Of course she didn't. And, of course, everybody believed her and not me. Why do you think that was?" He glared at her. He was going to force this issue.

"What?"

"Why did everybody believe what she said?"

"Because..." She hesitated. She couldn't quite bring herself to come right out and say what they had all said in those days.

But he could. "Because of the image that everyone already had of me. Right? I was already considered a juvenile delinquent. It just seemed like something a guy like Kimo Caine would do. Right?"

She nodded slowly, wishing she could see his eyes in the dark. "Yes. It did."

He swore softly, and then he laughed, but the sound held little humor. "Well, guess what. Kimo Caine didn't do it. The one time I slept with Amy, high as I was, I used a condom."

Taylor blinked, but he didn't give her time to react to that. "Did Amy ever have that baby?" he demanded.

Taylor thought for a second and shook her head. "No. She had a miscarriage."

He laughed again. "She was never pregnant." He faced her. "Don't you get it? She was never pregnant. She made the whole thing up when she was trying to blackmail me into going with her. And everyone believed her and didn't believe a word I said."

Taylor turned away, shivering. She knew what he was trying to prove here, but she didn't know how much of what he said she could believe. There was one thing she *did* know. She couldn't think about him sleeping with other women, even so long ago. Something stark and primeval rose in her at the thought. She wanted to find Amy Fosselburg and scratch her eyes out.

But no, she couldn't be thinking that way. He was nothing to her. Nothing. And he had to stay that way.

"Let's get back," she said, her voice muffled, and she turned to head for the house. She stumbled in the dark, stubbing her toe on a rock, and before he realized what he was doing, he reached out to steady her.

Only he didn't stop there. Somehow, he couldn't. Somehow, his arms just kept sliding around her. She slipped so easily into his embrace, as though it was meant to be. And this time she didn't say, "Don't touch." This time she didn't say anything at all.

His hands glided down and there was a breast, free and soft beneath the filmy fabric of her gown, and there was her spine, each vertebra a tiny bump, right down to the tailbone, right down to her rounded . . .

He tightened, hardened, and wanted her like he'd never wanted anything else. The shock of that wave of desire stunned him, and he dropped his arms, stepping away from her as though she was too hot to handle.

Now what had he gotten himself into? Not only did he want to prove to her what a great guy he was, he wanted to prove some other things, too. Things he had no business thinking about. On a certain level, he felt a sense of animal satisfaction in it, on another, he felt completely disgusted with himself.

She hadn't said a word through all this, hadn't pulled away. And she was still standing there as though she was dazed. His arms around her, his hands on her body, had felt like something calling from another world, like heaven, like hell. She shouldn't feel like this. It wasn't right. She was Tom's wife. She couldn't . . . wouldn't . . .

"You shouldn't have done that," she said dully. "I told you . . ."

"I . . . I'm sorry, Taylor. I didn't mean to do that. It just happened."

She shook her head. "It can't happen again." Suddenly she was furious with him. "You bastard, how could you do that? Don't you have any feelings for Tom? Didn't you listen to what I said? Tom is the only man I've ever had and he's the only man I'll ever have. How could you do this to me?"

Mack wasn't sure what he'd done. He frowned at her, hurt and sick that he'd put himself in the position of the bad boy once again. "I didn't do anything to you, Taylor."

But he had. She knew it, and it scared her silly.

"I've got to get out of here," she muttered, turning and beginning to walk quickly to the house. "Don't touch me."

"I'm not going to touch you," he insisted, falling in step beside her. But he wanted to touch her more than he wanted to breathe. And what was more, he knew she wanted it, too. Why couldn't she admit it?

They went into the house and he reached out and grabbed her arm. "Taylor . . ."

"No," she whispered fiercely, knowing all the while that refusing him was the hardest thing she'd done in a long, long time. "Leave me alone."

"Taylor, don't try to pretend with me. I've known you too long."

"I'm Tom's wife," she insisted, closing her eyes and shaking her head. "Tom's wife."

He dropped his hand, anger spilling out. "Go back and sleep with your memories, Taylor," he said cruelly. "They must make a wonderfully cold bed."

Turning on his heel, he left her there and went to his own room, shutting the door with a sense of finality.

Taylor stood in the hall, hardly breathing. She thought of him, of him dropping his clothes to the floor, of him sliding into bed, and she ached inside. Tears began to form in her eyes, but she blinked them back. This was the path she had chosen. Silently, she padded down the hall and went to bed.

Six

Breakfast was frigid. Mack felt as though an icy wind had blown in from Alaska, just for him. Taylor was polite, and she made him toast and eggs, but whenever his eyes met hers, the evidence that she was still angry was abundantly clear.

"I suppose my next move should be to get out and look this place over," he said as he finished eating. "Get a layout of the land."

She nodded, working hard to avoid his gaze. She refused to be embarrassed about last night, but that didn't mean she was proud of how she'd acted. She needed time to think, and the best thing would be to get him out of here for now. She was still angry, but she wasn't as sure she was justified in that anger. There were moments when she wasn't really sure if she was angry at him . . . or at herself.

"You'd better go on horseback," she said. "That's the best way to see everything."

"Horseback?" He grimaced. "Like...riding a horse, you mean?"

"Go on out to the stables," she said calmly. "Josi will get Solomon ready for you. He's a little ornery, but he's the biggest horse we've got. And you're a pretty big guy."

"Uh-huh." He nodded and grimaced. "Uh, what exactly do you mean by ornery?"

She glanced into his face. "You do ride horseback, don't you?"

"I have ridden." It had never been one of his favorite things, although he didn't want to admit that at the moment. "It's been a while. If it's anything like riding a bicycle..."

She looked at him as though he'd suddenly lost his training wheels. "It's nothing at all like riding a bicycle." Then she realized what he meant. "Oh, you mean you'll remember how."

"Hopefully." On the other hand, maybe he wouldn't. Maybe the horse would throw him over a cliff and he would die. That was a pretty good possibility. But how could he tell her that? Besides, the way she felt about him right now, if he brought up that prospect, she'd probably just smile and say, "Why not take our wildest horse? You're man enough. Aren't you, Mack?" No, he'd keep his misgivings to himself.

He wasn't angry at her any longer. In fact, after their last confrontation of the night, he'd put his head on his pillow and slept like a baby. No dreams. And when he'd awakened, he knew something that must have settled in his mind while he slept. There was going to be a romance here after all. Nothing permanent. Nothing serious. But he'd dreamed about Taylor for too long to let this opportunity pass. She would come around soon enough.

Right now, she was looking at the sky. It was clear over-head, but angry thunderclouds were gathering around the peaks of the neighboring mountains.

"Looks like we're in for some rain today," she com-mented. "Take along a rain slicker. There are some in the stable storeroom. And be careful. Solomon tends to spook if there's lightning."

Spook. Mack licked his lips and smiled, but he wasn't feeling very jolly. He wasn't sure, but he thought that when a horse was spooked, it bucked like a son of a gun and then took off for places unknown with the hapless rider—if he was still on board after the horse had tried every method of dislodging him known to man or beast—clinging to his neck in terror. It looked to be a real fun morning.

But a man had to do what a man had to do. Even if there was a horse involved. He went to his room and dressed, taking along the knife in his boot but leaving behind the re-volver. On a beautiful day like this, he didn't want to think it was going to be necessary.

The horse looked bigger and bigger the closer he got. And those huge teeth . . . He swung up on the giant animal okay. It was holding on that was going to present a problem. Still, he smiled gamely and waved goodbye and took off with the scent of morning in his head, and felt pretty good about it.

Taylor stood watching him go and frowned. It was pretty obvious he was no horseman. Maybe she should go along with him. But there was no way she could do that now. Ryan needed a ride to school and she had too much housework and a pile of paperwork to get through. Turning away, she left Mack to his fate.

But try as she would, she couldn't get him out of her mind. Funny how he'd been there in the back of her thoughts all these years, and now that he'd come home and she was really getting to understand him, it seemed as though she'd always known him, as though he'd never been gone, as though they'd been close even in high school, when the truth was, they'd barely spoken to one another.

She tried to push away the cobwebs and misconceptions the years could spin and see him as she had really seen him back then. She'd always been Tom's girl. But she'd always been fascinated by that bad boy, Kimo Caine. And scared of him at the same time.

Tom had been safe and right for her. Everyone had always admired Tom. He was the bright, all-American boy who always said the right thing and had the right manners. He and Kimo were like night and day. And she'd been attracted to both of them.

Now she knew Mack and she was beginning to think appearances were very deceiving. From what she could see, he wasn't a bad boy at all. Of course, he wasn't a boy any longer. But people didn't usually change that much. She'd seen a man who was good and kind and funny and compassionate. Why hadn't she seen that in him before? Funny— it seemed almost the flip side of what Tom had been. He had seemed so good, and yet, when you really got to know him...

But she mustn't let herself think about that. She always had to remember that Ryan needed to think his father had been everything that was wonderful. She couldn't ever slip up.

She was just putting the clothes into the drier about an hour later when she heard tires on gravel. Coolly slamming the drier door, she reached for the shotgun and moved swiftly to the kitchen porch, ready for anything.

Ready for anything threatening, at any rate. What she wasn't quite prepared for was to find the smiling faces of friends beaming at her from her front yard.

"Hi." Marge Washington waved from the driver's window of a station wagon, her head of dark curls bouncing in the sunlight.

"Hi." Two other women Taylor quickly recognized as Sherry Tanaka and Deb Tatiero hopped out of the car and waved, too.

Taylor frowned. Now what in the world were they doing here? She put down the shotgun and welcomed them in, mentally going over the beverage possibilities in her refrigerator as they filed into her kitchen.

"Well, it's nice to see you," she told them as they stood around and grinned at her. "Are you, uh, here for anything special?"

"Well, say, Taylor," Deb, the tall blond spokeswoman for the group said accusingly, "you never show up at the History Society meetings anymore, and you haven't been to our last three first-Tuesday-of-the-month luncheons, so we decided to get ourselves out here and see what was up."

Taylor stared at their smiling faces, a frown knitting her brows. Something didn't ring true. Sure, she'd known these women forever, or at least since high school. But they'd never been among her best friends, never the chatty sort of pals who dropped in on each other. She didn't think Deb had ever cared before whether she lived or died. So what made the difference now?

"How about some papaya juice?" she asked. "I'm afraid that's all I've got to offer right now."

Papaya juice—not a universal favorite. But all three women nodded happily and plopped themselves down at her kitchen table. Taylor poured out three glasses of the pinkish liquid and sat down to join them, still mystified.

However, she was not to be left in the dark for much longer. They chatted for a few moments about inconsequential happenings in the neighborhood, and then Deb got down to brass tacks.

"Okay," she said at last, craning her neck to see as far into the rest of the house as she could. "We know you've got him here somewhere. Where is he? Where are you hiding him?''

''Who?'' For a fraction of a second, Taylor really didn't realize who they were talking about. Her ignorance was swept away in an instant.

''Kimo Caine, of course,'' whispered Sherry Tanaka, talking low and looking over her shoulder as though she expected him to burst out of the broom closet at any moment. ''Lani told me he was staying with you.''

Taylor stared at her friends, aghast. ''Is that what you all came out here for? To see Kimo?''

''Sure.'' They were completely candid now. Marge leaned forward, her eyes bright with anticipation. ''Listen, Taylor, if you didn't have a crush on him in high school, you must have been the only one.''

''You could have knocked me over with a palm frond when Lani told me she'd seen him,'' Sherry gushed, smoothing her silver-blond bob into place. ''She said, 'Yeah, Mom, he's an old guy, but he's really fine looking.' And that's when I knew I had to come take a look.''

''We want to see him,'' Deb insisted firmly. ''Where have you got him?''

Taylor gazed at the three of them in wonder. She wouldn't have believed it if she hadn't seen it with her own eyes. ''I haven't got him anywhere,'' she said at last. ''He's gone.''

Mack was almost enjoying the ride. True, horseback riding always turned out to be incredibly bumpy compared to what it looked like in Westerns, and this horse was no pussycat. They'd already had an argument or two over directions to be taken. But the air was so fresh, and the scenery so beautiful, he couldn't complain.

Much of the Taggert ranch was dry and flat as a California desert, with ancient lava flows running in fat black ribbons across the sandy dirt. But one corner of the land rose into a set of small mountains that was covered with greenery and laced with waterfalls. Mack was drawn to the area. It was more like the coast where he'd lived growing up.

There was a crack of thunder from the mountaintop across the valley and Mack tensed, expecting old Solomon to react. But the horse just plodded on, paying no visible attention.

That was a relief. "Good boy," Mack muttered, patting his brown neck. "Good boy. We'll make sure you get an extra oat for that one."

Another flash, closer and louder, and still the horse strolled along as though he hadn't heard a thing.

"There you go," Mack said, talking as much to himself as to the horse. "You've got a bad reputation, just like me. And based on just as little reality. Isn't that right, big guy?"

It was a lovely day, a great setting. The air was soft. The birds were singing. A nice breeze was fluttering the leaves on the nearby trees. And suddenly, from out of a stand of greenery, a little cloud of butterflies spilled out, like flower petals thrown into the wind.

Maybe there was something threatening about those butterflies that Mack didn't see. Or maybe it was just that on top of the thunder and the birds and the wind, the butterflies were the proverbial straw that broke the horse's back. Maybe. Whatever the case was, Solomon chose this moment to bolt.

He bolted clean, he bolted fast, he bolted very far away— and he left Mack behind, struggling and swearing in the dust.

Meanwhile, back at the house, the fan club was going over old memories.

"He hid in my bedroom once." Deb giggled and bounced in her chair, looking almost like the teenager she'd been seventeen years before.

"He what?" the other two cried.

Taylor didn't say a word. She was enduring this with about as much joy as a root canal. Didn't these women realize how silly they were being? They'd been sitting at her kitchen table for the last half hour, reminiscing about everything they could collectively remember about Kimo Caine. It had done no good to explain to them that he was Mack Caine now, that he was older and not at all the cocky youth they were remembering. They were living in the past.

"It was so incredible," Deb went on, swooning where she sat.

"What happened?" Marge demanded.

"Well . . . it was late one Saturday night. I was just about to fall asleep when there was this knocking on my window. I opened the shutters, and there he was."

Marge and Sherry bounced in their chairs, squealing. "What did you do? What did he say?"

Deb leaned across the table. "He said, 'Hi, kiddo. Mind if I come in for a while?' "

"And you let him?"

"Are you kidding? Of course I let him in. He swung in and closed the window. I could see the police car down the street, using the searchlight." She sighed, remembering. "He stayed about half an hour, waiting for the cops to give up. We sat on the floor of my room in the dark and he sang songs to me."

"Songs!" They were as excited as young girls again. "What songs? Did he have a good voice?"

"The best. He sang old rock and roll songs from the fifties. And then—he kissed me—" She shook her head as the other two squealed. "No, not like that. On the forehead, and then he thanked me and went right back out through the window again." She shrugged. "I never saw him again except at school. Sometimes he would smile at me. But that was all."

Taylor studied Deb with a frown while the others oohed and aahed over her story. Running from the cops sounded true to form, but how could that wild boy Kimo Caine have been so sweet and gentle to her? He sounded more like the Mack Caine she knew today. Funny.

She thought of the night before, when he'd almost kissed her, and now she wished she'd let him. He'd been angry at the way she'd rejected him. Would he try again?

"He was so cute," Sherry said on a sigh, her eyes dreamy, and Taylor frowned again. This was Sherry Hall, the militant feminist who once gave a rousing speech at assembly about how women didn't really need men in their lives and would be better off living in communes gated against them. Granted, she'd toned down over the years, but if she'd had a crush on Mack way back then, what had all that other gibberish been about?

"He went out with my best friend, Tammy," Marge said.

"No! Really?"

Marge nodded. "When I heard he was back, I called her. She's in Seattle now. Has five kids and a husband she adores. But she screamed when I said he was back in town. She couldn't help it. She went wild."

"He was so dreamy." Deb sighed.

Taylor rose from her seat in one quick lunge and started for the bathroom.

"Where are you going?" Marge called after her.

"To be sick," she whispered to herself, but aloud she only said, "I'll be right back."

"Don't forget, you promised we could see him."

"You can see him," she said, impatience getting the better of her. "He should be back soon." She gazed out the window in the direction he had left earlier. "Be back soon, Mack," she muttered to herself. "I can't take much more of this."

* * *

It wasn't likely Mack was going to comply with those wishes. Not only had he lost his horse, he'd been sidetracked. Walking was hot work, and as his path took him by Taylor's nice little river, he was more and more tempted, and finally succumbed. Stripping his clothes off and leaving them on a rock beside the water, he'd jumped in. Right now, he was floating on his back and thinking he really was in paradise.

From where he swam he could look down on miles and miles of beautiful landscape that looked as though it could have come straight from the surface of the moon. Looking up, he stared at the mountains, shrouded right now by a storm cloud that was doubtless pouring water down the slopes, while he was in the sunshine, at the foot of a little waterfall, surrounded by jungle greenery. It was the best of all worlds. In some ways he wished he could stay here forever.

The cattle he could see grazing had to be Bart's. And that brought the situation to mind. What was he going to do to help Taylor get that jerk off her back?

He hadn't quite figured out why Bart wanted the Taggert ranch. After all, the two ranches had existed side by side for generations. The Taggert ranch wasn't really big enough to interest Bart. Could there be more to it?

Now that he thought about it, there had been something in the way Bart had related to Taylor that had puzzled him at the time. The man had tried to bully her, it was true. But there had been more than intimidation in his manner. There was something else going on, something Taylor hadn't told him about. He couldn't quite put his finger on what it was, but he was going to have to get her to come clean before he would know for sure how to handle the situation.

Which reminded him, it was about time to get back. It was going to be a long walk. If he expected to get any lunch today, he'd better get started. He had just taken a fix on where his clothes were stashed and begun to breaststroke toward the rock when a strange roaring caught him by surprise. He stopped and looked toward the waterfall, puzzled. When the wall of water came shooting over the top, he was totally unprepared.

"Stupid," he was telling himself even as the water tumbled him against the rocks. "Stupid." He knew about flash floods. He knew that if it rained in the mountains, the water had to come down somewhere. And yet the possibility of flooding hadn't even entered his mind.

He tried to right himself and smashed his hand against basalt with all its sharp edges. Swallowing a mouthful of water, he finally found his feet as the rush of the water began to die down a little. He pulled himself out and sat for a moment and caught his breath, then oriented himself. He was about one hundred yards downriver from where he'd started. He would have to make his way back on land. He didn't trust the water at the moment.

He felt a little silly walking naked, but what the heck—there was no one around. He hadn't seen another person since he'd left the stables that morning. The only people he was likely to see were the men working Taylor's cattle or the men working Bart's. And if he saw them, he could bear the humiliation. It was no big deal.

It was no big deal when the walk was short and the prospect of getting dressed again imminent. What *was* a big deal was realizing he had found the rock where his clothes were supposed to be—and realizing with shock that they weren't there anymore.

It took a moment for the truth to register, and when it did, he scrambled along the riverbank, sure he would find his jeans at least caught somewhere along the shore. But finally he had to face reality. The clothes were gone. The only things left were his wide leather belt and his boots. He was stuck out on Taylor's ranch with no horse, stark naked.

He stood for a long moment staring at his few remaining possessions. There had to be a catch. Somehow, something had to come to his rescue. This just plain couldn't be happening.

A bird cried. The river returned to its usual gentle flow. And still he stood there, holding the belt in his hand, trying to figure out how to make a piece of clothing out of it.

There was no way. It had to be faced. And he had to get back. He could wait out here until the cows came home—so to speak—and that wouldn't change the facts. He was naked. Except for a belt and boots.

He stared at the belt again, turning it over and over in his hands. Well, what was he going to do with the damn thing— wear it on his head? Carry it in his teeth? Might as well put it on, along with the boots, which he was grateful he had. Walking back barefoot would have brought on a whole new set of problems. Okay, he was ready to go. Sort of. He took off through the brushy area and came out in the flat land.

Now he really felt silly. A grown man, buck naked in cowboy boots with a tooled leather belt around his hips, walking along through the Hawaiian countryside. This had to be a dream. A very, very bad dream.

Somehow he was going to have to get into Taylor's house without being seen. Especially by Taylor. Right now he didn't see how he was going to do it. But something would come to mind. It had to.

Seven

Taylor looked out the window and saw Solomon coming back with an empty saddle. She jumped up from the table and went outside, her heart in her throat. Forgetting all about her visitors, she headed for the stable.

"What happened?" she cried to Josi as she ran up.

The elderly man looked at her, alarmed. "I don't know, Miz Taggert. I just looked out here and there was Solomon and I—"

She brushed past him and went to the horse, looking for clues, studying the saddle and bridle, feeling his legs. There was nothing, no wound, nothing torn, nothing missing. She couldn't tell what had happened. But it was a good bet Mack had been thrown.

"Damn," she bit out emphatically. She shouldn't have let him go alone. She'd seen what a lousy horseman he was. "Damn, damn, damn!" This was her fault. She should never have let him go that way.

"Okay, Solomon," she said firmly. "You're going to take me back to him, you idiot horse."

She swung onto his back, but before she could take off, the three women came running from the house, puffing with the effort.

"What is it?" Marge asked anxiously. "What's happened?"

"Is it something to do with Kimo?" Deb asked suspiciously. "You're going to him, aren't you? Why can't we come along?"

Taylor had to leash her instinctive response and try to manufacture some politeness. Why couldn't they just go home and leave her alone?

"Mack seems to have been thrown," she said evenly. "I'm going out to look for him. He can't be far, and I'm sure I'll be back in no time. If you come along, it will just take that much longer. You all go back to the house and wait."

They milled together, muttering and throwing dark looks Taylor's way, but in the end they took her advice and began to trudge to the house. Taylor looked after them, exasperated. They were acting like silly teenage groupies of some rock star.

"Grow up already," she muttered, but she had other things to think about. In another moment, she was off, fear beating like a wild thing in her chest. What if he'd been badly hurt? He could have broken a leg. He could have hurt his back. He might have hit his head on a rock. A thousand disasters seemed almost inevitable. If anything bad had happened to him . . .

Bad things could happen so easily. She remembered the day she'd said goodbye to Tom and sent him off to go hunting. It had been a day just like any other. Better, in fact. They had laughed over breakfast, laughed at something Ryan had done. And just before he'd left, he'd kissed her.

That had been something to hold on to during the dark time after she had to admit to herself that he was gone. At least they'd parted as friends. But he'd slipped away so easily....

No. She couldn't think about that. She had to find Mack quickly. If he needed help, she would be there to give it to him. If he needed a ride back, she would provide that. She refused to consider any other option.

Mack saw her coming and swore obscenely. He couldn't let her see him this way. It was just too humiliating. Quickly, he slipped into a cluster of flame trees and elephant ear plants, whose leaves came up at least as high as his chin in most places. She was riding his old friend Solomon and coming slowly, peering into the jungle, obviously looking for him. It went against his character to do this, but he had to hide. There was no way he was presenting himself like some giant Puss-in-Boots for her inspection. He would just lay low and wait for her to pass.

She came closer. He could see her clearly. He held his breath, and for the first time in years he actually prayed. In another moment she would go on by and he could continue toward the house. If, for a change, luck was with him, he might be able to make it back before she returned. No one would be home. He could run into the empty house and no one would see him. Right now, that was about the best he could hope for.

Another half a minute and she would be gone. Just another minute. Just another...

Solomon had come to a stop and was staring into the greenery, his velvet nose pointing straight at where Mack was hidden. Every muscle in Mack's body sagged. Damn that animal. Could they sense when you hated them, like dogs did? Must be. But what had he ever done to this one to make him so mean?

Taylor was peering in through the leaves, trying to separate the different shades of green and searching for a color that didn't blend, looking more for a body on the ground than anything else. Solomon was a good old horse. Sometimes he actually seemed to sense what people wanted from him. Right now she had a feeling he was showing her something. Wait. Was that a human face in between those huge elephant ear leaves?

Mack swore again. It was all over.

"Mack?" Taylor shaded her eyes and stared right at him, relief sweeping through her in waves. "Is that you?"

He groaned. "Damn it all," he added, all hope gone.

"Mack, what are you doing in there?" From where she sat she couldn't see anything but his eyes and a bit of his hair. But her heart was beating a wild pattern in her chest and she felt light-headed. It *was* him. And he was okay. It startled her a little to realize how much she cared about that.

She started to swing off the horse but he stopped her with a quick warning. "Stop. Don't get down, Taylor. I'll turn and run if you do."

"What?" She settled in the saddle, perplexed. "What on earth are you talking about?"

Oblivious to her concerns, Mack wished he could fall into a hole in the earth and never come back. He looked hopefully at his feet, but nothing happened.

"Listen, Taylor," he told her sorrowfully. "Why don't you just go on and look for me. Pretend you haven't a clue as to where I really am. Just take a little ride to the end of your ranch..."

He was talking like a crazy person. She frowned, staring harder, leaning forward in the saddle. "Mack, what are you doing back there? Are you hurt? Why don't you come out?"

He had a very bad feeling about this. She wasn't going to go away and leave him alone, was she? "No, I'm not hurt. The truth is . . . I'm hiding back here, Taylor."

This was insane. She shook her head. Was there something she just didn't get? "Why are you hiding?" she asked carefully.

He sighed. He was going to have to come clean. This was the worst nightmare he'd ever had. Why couldn't he wake up? "Because, at the present time...I don't have any clothes on."

"Oh." She sat and thought about that for a moment, amazed. No, it still didn't make any sense. "What are you talking about? Where are your clothes?"

"It's a very long story. I'll tell you all about it sometime. In the meantime, why don't you just go along, have a nice ride, pretend you never saw me and give me a chance to make it back to the house with some sort of dignity intact."

She shook her head. It was finally sinking in that he wasn't kidding. "You're really naked? You don't have any clothes on at all?" This was definitely bizarre. And, she was beginning to realize, pretty funny. She grinned. "No clothes at all?"

"No," he replied with barely leashed impatience. "A flash flood took them away. Okay?"

She had to hold the laugh back. Some little instinct told her he wasn't going to appreciate the humor for a good long time. "Oh, you were swimming?"

"The lady is quick, I'll give her that. Yes, I was swimming. And you can stop laughing now."

She chuckled. She couldn't hold it back. She loved this. Mack Caine, Mr. Cool, Mr. Tough Guy, Mr. Always-in-Control, stuck naked out in the wilderness. It was too delicious. "I can't help it."

Of course she couldn't help it. Mack knew that. But that didn't stop him from hating her for it. "I don't suppose you've got any extra clothing with you? Nothing I could use?''

"No. Sorry." She'd worn a sun suit. Nothing extra. And the saddle blanket old Solomon used was specially made for its task, and torn and threadbare anyway, completely useless for covering the normal male. Besides, she didn't want to help him out. For once, she was the one who was comfortable and confident and he was the one in an awkward position. She wanted to savor it while she could. She smiled and waited to see what his next suggestion was going to be.

"Okay, Taylor, this is serious. If you could just go on and take a ride and give me time to sneak into the house..."

She was already shaking her head. "There's no way you can do that without being seen."

"By who? Josi? I can handle that."

"That's not all." How was she going to break this to him gently? She swallowed her laughter and forced a straight face. "You've got visitors."

He froze, his fingers clutching a larger leaf stem. "Visitors?" he said, his voice slightly husky. "What are you talking about?"

"Three old friends from high school. They came to see you." The laugh wouldn't be contained any longer and it came out as a smothered giggle. "Only they had no idea how much they might get to see."

"Cute." He could see she was really enjoying this. She had absolutely no compassion. Weren't women supposed to be sensitive to the feelings of others? He gritted his teeth. "We need someone with your sense of humor at a time like this," he said, sarcasm dripping from his words.

She struggled and managed to cut back the giggles. "Come on now. It's not all that serious."

He was about to point out that her opinion would probably be a bit different if she was the one without clothes, but he stopped himself. They were straying from the point. He had to get this other stuff cleared up. "What do you mean, friends from high school? I don't have any friends from high school."

She smiled. "Maybe I should call them admirers. You remember Sherry Tanaka, used to be Sherry Hall. And Marge Washington, used to be Marge Hinada. And Deb Tatiero, used to be Deb Carter."

Sherry they had talked about the day before. She was Lani's mother. The other two didn't ring any large bells, but they did tickle the edges of his memory. Whatever, they were an audience, and an audience was something he didn't need. He frowned, knowing he couldn't be fierce enough to scare anybody while he was naked like this. "Tell them to go away."

She shook her head. "Can't," she said without a whole lot of remorse. "I've been trying to get them to go away all morning. They've been camped out in my kitchen, waiting for you to come back."

Come on, this *had* to be a nightmare. This couldn't be for real. He'd never had a worse day, and that included a few with harrowing escapes from gangs of drug runners. Oh, for the good old days, when only his life was in danger, not his image and self-esteem. He slapped a large mosquito, which had just landed on his arm, and grimaced. "What do they want with me?"

"What do you think they want? They want to rekindle old memories and relight the fires on crushes of days gone by."

He groaned. "Oh, this ought to do it. Once I come in from horseback riding without any clothes on, I'll be a laughingstock."

"It'll be the top story at the next reunion," she promised with a grin. "Your place in the history of this side of the island will be secure."

He broke off a leaf and crushed it. "No it won't. Because I won't go back in front of them. I'll stay here forever if I have to."

She laughed. He sounded a lot like Ryan when he was pouting. Enough of this already. "Come on out. I'll take you back."

"Not in front of that gang of women. They'd tear me limb from limb."

"What's the alternative? You want to stay out here and let the insects eat you alive?"

"No." He slapped at another mosquito. "Hey, here's an idea. You go back and get me some clothes and bring them to me."

She could do that, but she foresaw some obstacles. "I'd be bringing back more than the clothes. The troika would be sure to tag along this time. They were already losing trust in me. They think I've got you hidden away so I can keep you all to myself."

"Interesting thought." He actually found himself smiling at her. "I wouldn't mind going into that idea further— once I get some clothes on and don't feel like something out of a bad porno movie."

She smiled back. He really was being remarkably good-humored about this. Tom would have been having a cow by now. "Okay, here's a better idea. It's actually workable. You come on out and get up behind me on Solomon. We'll run over to the workman's cottage Josi has set up at the edge of the meadow. He sometimes keeps some extra clothes out there. You'll grab something, put it on, and then we'll go face the fearsome females."

"No good." He shook his head.

"Why not?"

"I still have to appear like a naked idiot before you. I can't do that, Taylor. It's just impossible."

She shook her head. Men and their egos. "Don't be ridiculous. I've been married and I have a son. I've seen men naked before."

"Taylor..."

"And I'm sure other women have seen you naked before. Come on, Mack, don't be such a baby."

It took another five minutes to coax him out. He tried to be nonchalant, but failed miserably. He was embarrassed. Who wouldn't be? But if it had to be done, t'were best done quickly. So he came out from behind his elephant ear protection and walked with his head held high, feeling as though he was mounting the stairs to the guillotine.

Taylor tried to act nonchalant, too, but she didn't do much better than he did. There was a strange buzzing in her ears the whole time. And she kept hearing herself saying, "I've seen men naked before."

Yes, she'd seen men naked. But she'd never seen *this* man naked. The moment she did, something seemed to happen inside her, something she hadn't expected at all. The middle section of her body seemed to cave in, as though the air had suddenly been drawn out of it like a balloon, as though she'd gone over a mountain on a roller coaster and now there was no bottom to her fall. She'd meant to look away. She'd meant to avert her eyes. She never, ever meant to look at him. But once she'd begun, she couldn't stop.

It wasn't fair. Naked men were supposed to look vulnerable, pale, sort of puny and inconsequential. He didn't look that way at all. The muscles on his shoulders were stunningly defined, and his stomach looked like a washboard. As for the rest of him—she could hardly breathe after glancing there. He looked like some Viking warrior or Polynesian god of fire, or maybe a sculpture by Michelangelo—strong, invincible and sexy as hell.

You're so beautiful!

Dear Lord, had she said it aloud? No. Thank God. She'd only thought it. Taking a deep breath, she steadied herself. This was going to be very interesting. And not a little frightening.

And yet, she wasn't really frightened. She was excited. Anticipation tingled through her. It was then she realized that she'd been on some kind of high ever since Mack had arrived. It was him—*he* did this to her. He was like an intoxicant. She'd better be very careful how far she let this go.

She managed to pull her gaze away from him, looking down and moving forward in the saddle in anticipation of him coming aboard, and her gaze fell on something yellow tucked into the pouch.

Mack caught sight of it at the same time.

"The rain slicker." He grabbed at it, relief pouring through him. "You were holding out on me, lady."

"I forgot about it." She watched, just barely suppressing the giggles while he slipped the poncholike thing over his head. It covered his shoulders nicely, but only fell to about ten inches above his knees.

"This is hardly the answer to my prayers," he said bitterly, looking down.

She couldn't help it. He looked so forlorn. She burst out laughing and he looked up, his eyes brimming with humor. "You're going to pay for this, Taylor," he warned, taking the hand she held out to help him and swinging up behind her. "I'll make you sorry you ever laughed at me."

"Ooh, a scary naked guy," she teased, then ducked as he made a mock grab for her.

"You'd better watch out," he told her. "I'm right behind you, you know. I may be a ridiculous naked guy in a yellow rain slicker, but I'm watching every move you make."

She laughed and started Solomon off at a nice trot. Mack was holding on to the saddle, not her, but she still tingled with a sense of his nearness. Rain slicker or not, he was basically naked. And she was basically electrified by the whole situation.

"How close do we have to pass by the house?" he asked, still worried about his potential audience.

"They'll be able to see us from the house, if they're watching. We'll have to chance it."

He swore softly, then laughed. "Do you know how silly I feel?"

"You're in a silly situation," she told him quite seriously. "But you're not a silly man. It won't last."

They were both silent for a few moments after that, she wishing she hadn't said it, he wishing he knew for sure what she meant by it. Her hair blew across his face, filling his senses with the scent of roses. He closed his eyes and forced himself not to want her. This seminakedness was too awkward and much too embarrassing. He wished he was anywhere but here.

"What do you think?" he said heartily in her ear. "Is there more rain coming?"

"What?" Her mind was still groggy from the effect he had on her. He was almost naked and beautiful and he was sitting right behind her. She felt very, very hot, as though she was running a fever and under a hot pad at the same time.

"The weather, Taylor. I'm trying to make conversation here."

"Oh. Of course. Uh... there seems to be a storm cloud over the horizon."

"Yes." That just about exhausted that topic. "Read any good books lately?"

"Oh, Mack!"

"I'm just trying to concentrate our minds on something other than..."

She glanced back and her smile was mischievous. "Than what?"

His fingers were suddenly in the hair at the back of her neck, tangling in her curls, and his face was close behind. "Than this insane desire I have to throw you down on the leaves and ravish you," he murmured in her ear.

"Don't be ridiculous," she said, but she didn't pull away.

She hadn't pulled away. Something wild began to race through his blood.

"I'm not being ridiculous," he murmured. "I'm being human."

Last night she'd warned him not to touch her. Now it was too late. The reaction she'd been so afraid of had already begun. She closed her eyes, savoring the warmth of his breath on her neck.

It wouldn't hurt to enjoy him for just a moment, would it? She leaned into his embrace as though she was drugged, letting his arms tighten around her, letting him nibble at her ear, letting the tiny, delicious shudders begin to roll through her body in waves. It had been so long since she'd felt loved.

"Taylor," he murmured against her neck, "you taste so good."

She seemed to melt against him and his arms went around her, his hands sliding up to find her breasts. He could feel the nipples beneath the thin cloth, hardening against the palms of his hands. He could hardly believe he was actually touching her this way. Maybe this was all still a part of his nightmare. Or had his nightmare turned into a wonderful dream?

She didn't stop him. She couldn't stop him. Instead, she turned her head and let his mouth take hers, a quick caress of lips and tongue that filled her with a longing that was a lot like butterscotch syrup, thick and golden and delicious. But it couldn't last.

"We're almost in sight of the house," she told him, drawing away reluctantly.

He let her go, but he stayed close, his hands on her waist, circling her as though to keep her real.

"We'll make this as fast as we can," Taylor called back, stirring Solomon into a gallop. "Hold on."

He could see the house on the crest of the hill. He smiled and waved, just in case they were watching. And then they'd disappeared into a clump of trees and the little workman's hut was dead ahead.

"Quick," cried Taylor, laughing as she pulled Solomon to a stop. "Get inside."

They both slipped off the horse and raced for the hut, making it in a dead heat, laughing and clinging together as they made it to safety. Mack's dark eyes met hers and held, and as their laughter died away, he reached out to tilt up her chin and cover her mouth with his, drawing gently from her sweetness.

She couldn't help but kiss him back. She was standing here with an almost naked man, and she knew this went against all her principles, against everything she'd said the night before, and still, she felt the most overwhelming sense of happiness.

"You'd better hurry and get some clothes on," she murmured against his lips.

"Not yet," he whispered. "Not yet."

He let her go only long enough to slip out of the rain slicker and then he had her in his arms again. His hand found the zipper at the back of her jumpsuit and in a moment it had fallen to the floor with a sound as soft as the flutter of an angel's wing. She knew she should stop him, but she didn't care, not right now. All her fear was gone. He was big and bold and he would fill her with his strength, and that was what she needed. That, and the caress of his hand as he pushed her hair back to let him kiss her ear, the tantalizing heat of his tongue, the hard pressure of his body against her breasts.

He kissed her again and again, wanting to devour her, afraid of hurting her with the intensity of his need. This was something he had dreamed about from the time he had first had this kind of dream. He wasn't sure if he still wasn't dreaming. Did any woman really have breasts this soft, this high, with nipples that stood so tight, so hard? Looking at her made him throb with desire, touching her made that need almost pain. Sweet agony. He finally knew what that meant.

And so did she. Her body had been made for his touch. She arched to it, sighed and gasped when he responded with his fingers, his lips and tongue. Her arms wrapped around his neck and she pulled him even closer, finding his warm mouth with her own, digging her fingers into his thick hair. She was ready for this. She felt as though she'd been waiting for this all her life.

For just a moment, he drew back. "Are you sure, Taylor?" he asked, his voice husky with desire. "You know we don't have..."

"Hush." She kissed him quickly, stopping his words. "Don't talk."

She didn't want to talk. Talking would make her think. And if she thought this through, she wouldn't do it.

He tugged off her panties and lay her down on the clean straw. The dappled light from the broken window fell on her skin, spreading silver on her body. He touched the places were the sunlight was, and then he touched more, his hand trailing fire, his lips finding her most sensitive places, and she writhed beside him, responding to his every move, breathing quickly, urgently, demandingly.

Now there was no more time for reluctance. Like the flash flood that had swept him off his feet earlier that day, the power of his feelings and his need were becoming too strong to hold back.

"Taylor?" he asked, agony in his voice.

"Yes," she told him quickly. "Oh, yes, Mack."

His body was hard and hot and exciting as it came on top of her, smooth as marble, warm as the sun. She took him eagerly, not sure what to expect, but beyond caring. She needed him badly, all of him, right now.

He came inside her and she felt an explosion of joy so intense it led right into the roller coaster ride, going faster and faster, higher and higher, through the clouds, into sensations beyond her comprehension, until she cried out in sweet anguish and clung to him as though he was her last refuge on earth.

He held her tightly, eyes closed. This wasn't just another dream. This was real. No dream had ever been this good. Nothing had ever been this good. Taylor, for this moment at least, was his.

"Mack?" Taylor questioned, needing to see his reaction in his eyes.

He opened them and looked at her, and suddenly they both smiled.

"You're not sorry?" he whispered, brushing her hair with a tender gesture.

She shook her head, but she couldn't speak. How could she explain to him that what they had just done had been the most wonderful experience of her life? With Tom, it had never been so full, so intense.... But she didn't want to think about Tom. Tom was the father of her son. She would never, ever tell anyone anything bad about him.

She had made love with Mack Caine. She wanted to stretch like a cat before a fireplace, luxuriating in the feel of it. How could it have been so good? How could he have been so good to her? He was supposed to be bad, and dangerous, and rough. But his lovemaking had been the most tender and sensitive she'd ever experienced. It didn't fit with the image. Nothing seemed to make sense anymore. But she didn't care. As long as he held her.

"Listen."

They both held very still. There was a strange sound coming from not very far away.

"Horses," Taylor said, and they both scrambled to their feet and went to the window.

In the distance they could see three horses leaving the stables, heading out in the direction Taylor had taken when she'd set off to find Mack.

"It's your friends," Taylor said, laughing. "They didn't see us. They've gone off to look for you themselves."

"Good," he murmured, kissing her ear again. "That gives us more time."

She looked at him in surprise. "Time for what?"

But he didn't have to explain. She got it quickly enough. And in a moment, they were on the straw again, setting off a new round of fireworks.

Eight

The ride to the house was very different. They took it slowly, meandering here and there, as though neither one of them really wanted to get back. Taylor was filled with a delicious lethargy, and Mack was feeling masculine and proud of himself. They had a special bond, but they both knew it wouldn't last, and they were hoping to put off breaking it as long as possible.

Dressed in a torn chambray shirt and an old baggy pair of jeans, Mack rode in front this time. Taylor rode behind him, her arms around him, her cheek against his back. She was having a hard time dealing with what she'd done. She'd made love with Mack Caine. And if the truth be known, she was half in love with him, too.

But who was he, this bad boy turned protector? She knew what she felt about him. She knew what she could know by looking into his eyes and feeling his touch. But she knew there was much, much more. She had to know more about him.

For starters, why was he considered so bad?

"What is the worst thing you've ever done?" she asked him.

He laughed. "Are you feeling guilty?" he teased.

She smiled dreamily. "Hardly. No, I'm just trying to understand . . . How did you first get the reputation for being such a bad guy? How did it all start?"

He shrugged. "I was probably a pretty rowdy kid." He hesitated for a moment. He'd never really analyzed it for anyone before. But there was something about Taylor that made him think she would listen and understand.

"I was the kind of kid who always got caught. If I was with a group of boys and we caused a commotion at the beach or at the movie theater, I was the one all the witnesses remembered. You know what I mean? Somehow I was never sneaky enough. So I was always the one who got nailed."

She nodded, remembering the skinny kid she'd known so many years ago. That was part of it. But wasn't there more?

"Then of course, there's always the Caine legacy," Mack added, as though he'd read her mind.

Well, that wasn't exactly what she'd meant. But it was an interesting angle. "What's that?"

"You never heard about my great-grandfather Morgan Caine, the pirate?"

"Oh, sure. I do know about him." She raised her head and grinned. "Everybody knows. That's part of your mystique."

He grimaced. "I didn't know I had 'mystique.'"

"Trust me." She laughed softly, thinking of the three women right now in hot pursuit of his bod. "You've got it."

"Well, old Morgan is part of the burden all us Caines have to bear. I've always known, right from the beginning, that I had a wild streak. Pirate blood. It's like I was born to be bad."

She frowned into the sun. "But that's not true. No one is born to be bad."

"You're right. I don't believe that stuff anymore. But I used to. And it probably had a lot to do with what I expected out of life for a long time. And how I acted."

They were at the stables, and she slid down reluctantly. He came down beside her and looked into her eyes. His were suddenly serious. Because this was the crux of it all. If he couldn't communicate this to her, everything else was a waste.

"I know now that I wasn't born to be bad, Taylor. I wasn't ever really bad, not like they used to say. I was just a normal kid. And I'm just a normal man."

It was important for him to believe that, but something in the way he said it made her think he was still trying to convince himself. "Do you really believe it?" she asked him softly.

"Yeah, I think I do." He frowned, still holding her gaze. Then something like pain shadowed his gaze. "The question is," he added softly, "do you?"

"Me?" She stepped back in surprise. "Well, of course."

He shook his head slowly, denying what she'd said. "You've always been sure I was an outlaw. I could see it in your eyes."

"No, Mack. That's not true."

She reached toward him, but a cloud had come into his gaze and he wasn't the same man she'd just made love with. He turned away, speaking to Josi, who had come out to take care of the horse, leaving her alone.

She crossed her arms over her chest and stood watching him, feeling very cold. She wanted to deny what he'd accused her of. And she would do so when given the chance. But a part of her had to admit, at least to herself, that he had a point. She had thought about him in those terms for a very long time. And it was true. She still wasn't sure she could trust him.

After all, she'd known Tom for years when she'd married him. And look at how that had turned out.

He turned and looked at her, but his gaze didn't invite a smile. "I'm going to run out to the airfield before those women get back," he said, and then he seemed to remember that he was supposedly working for her. "Unless you need me to stick around here for something."

She shook her head slowly. "No," she said simply. "You can go. Take my car."

He hesitated for a moment, then strode toward the house. Taylor stayed in the stables and spent some time fussing with the horses. She wanted him gone before she went back. She had too much to think about. She had to decide if she was going to let herself fall in love.

"Kimo Caine."

"That's me. Only nowadays I go by Mack."

The older man grinned and stuck out his hand. "Didn't recognize you the other day."

Bob Albright had taught him to fly. At one time, Mack had thought he was a god. "And you recognized me now?" Mack was still a little cynical after what had happened the last time he'd been at the airfield.

"Absolutely. I thought you looked familiar. I kept mulling it over yesterday, and finally, in the middle of dinner, it hit me. Kimo Caine! I yelled it out, right in the middle of the restaurant. Hey, it's good to see you." And his pale blue eyes seemed to be beaming with genuine emotion. "Been a long time."

Finally Mack let himself unbend enough to smile. "You got that right," he said.

They launched into a short explanation of what each had been doing for the past seventeen years, and then Bob added, "Hey, Bart Carlson's really interested in that PBY of yours."

Mack's dark eyes narrowed. "Yeah, I've heard."

Bob gestured toward the field. "He's out there looking it over right now."

"Is he? How convenient." Mack smiled to try to take the sarcasm out of his tone. "I guess I'd better go have a chat with the boy."

"You do that. But, hey, you come on back and talk some more, okay? It sure is good to see you."

The encounter with Bob had warmed him. It was nice to know someone remembered him fondly. But as he walked toward where his plane was parked, the warmth ebbed away. He could see Bart climbing all over the PBY. He had to hold back the anger that threatened. It would be best to approach this coolly.

He came to a stop beneath the ladder where Bart was clinging at the moment.

"Hello there, Bart," he said evenly. "Got your hands all over something else that belongs to me?"

The words surprised him as much as they must have surprised Bart. Taylor didn't exactly belong to him, did she? But that was how he felt about her. Still, it was a good thing she wasn't within earshot or she'd have killed him.

But Bart had heard, and he understood. His eyes were icy as he slid down the ladder and turned to face Mack where he stood waiting. There was a vein throbbing at his temple. If Mack wanted a fight, his face seemed to say, he was ready to give him one.

"Where do you get off coming back after seventeen years and thinking you can take over everything?" he demanded, standing tall and threatening, like a man who was accustomed to ordering people around, accustomed to grinding them into the dirt if necessary, just to prove his dominance. "Who the hell do you think you are?"

But Mack wasn't used to being ordered around, and he stood his ground, jaw jutting out, eyes hard and unrelenting. "I'm not taking over everything. I'm just protecting things I care about."

Bart's gaze raked over him as though Mack was something to be despised. "Since when has Taylor been yours?" he sneered.

Mack twitched. It was obviously going to take real effort not to lose his temper here. "I didn't say she was mine," he replied carefully.

Bart's nostrils flared. "You certainly implied it."

Keep cool, Mack, he was telling himself. Don't let this guy make a fool of you. It's not like the old days, when you were a teenager and Bart was in his twenties and already the richest, most powerful man in the area. Things were different now. Mack didn't get awed by that sort of thing any longer.

"Taylor has hired me," he said, choosing his words carefully, "and I figure that gives me certain proprietary rights."

Fire flashed in Bart's eyes. "Not to her it doesn't. Taylor Taggert's a wonderful woman. She deserves the best in life." He jabbed a finger in Mack's direction. "And that ain't you, Caine. And you know it." Bart's face was red with anger, and his voice was low and mean. "You'd best leave her alone, son. Take my advice, or you'll regret it."

His words had plenty of sting, but Mack was becoming immune. The more Bart blustered, the less he respected him. He even managed a smile in the face of the man's anger.

"Calm down, Bart. I agree with you one hundred percent. And bottom line, Taylor will make her own decisions. What you and I shout at each other won't matter a hill of beans."

Bart blinked, and strangely, did just as Mack suggested. He took a deep breath and his color began to return to normal, his stance losing its aggressive edge. And finally, he shrugged.

"You're right," he muttered. Turning, he gestured toward the plane. "This is what I'm here for anyway. I hear you own this little beauty. How much do you want for her?"

Mack looked at the aircraft he had so lovingly restored with his own two hands. Even if he was in the mood to get rid of her, Bart Carlson would be the last man he would give her to. "She's not for sale."

Bart moved impatiently. "Name your price, Caine. I'll give you whatever you want."

He shook his head. "I'm not selling her."

"You'll change your mind when you hear my offer."

Mack's smile had a deadly calm. "I don't think so. You can't buy everything, Bart. Some things are just not for sale."

Bart's anger was beginning to come back, but he seemed to know it would do him no good. He stood clenching and unclenching his hands for a moment, then turned to go, saying over his shoulder, "I want that beauty, Caine. And you know what? I always get what I want. That's just the way it is." He stopped and looked Mack full in the face. "There are two things I want very badly right now. And I aim to get both of them. So I guess you're just going to be out of luck. Get prepared to lose, Caine. It's just your destiny." He grinned and turned, whistling as he went.

Mack stared after him. Two things that he wanted—somehow he had a feeling he knew what those two things were. And they had very little to do with land. It was strange, really. The man who was supposedly so obsessed with getting the Taggert ranch in his possession hadn't said one word about it. But he'd sure said a lot about Taylor Taggert.

Taylor Taggert. He climbed into the plane and went directly to the cockpit. There were a couple of cables he wanted to replace. And he wanted to think. Working with his hands always made him think better.

He brought out the spool of cable and cut himself a length, then leaned down under the panel and began to detach the old one. But all the time he was thinking about Taylor, about how she'd felt in his arms, about how much he wanted her there again. He'd never expected to go this far with her. She'd lived in his dreams for so many years, it was hard to imagine her anywhere else. And there had been something so cool and reserved about her at first. But she'd been warm when he'd made love to her, warm and real and as responsive as any woman he'd ever known.

For a moment he thought about Jill, and then he realized he'd had to make a conscious effort just to conjure up her picture. Once it had haunted him all the time. Now he had to try to see her face. Silently, he grinned. Good. It was high time he got over her. Once he could honestly say he wished her happiness, he would know he was completely healed.

"Hey, Mack."

He jerked up, bumping his head, and turned to see Lani's bright face coming up the ladder. Dressed in coveralls, as usual, she looked like a boy at first glance, a young, slender apprentice mechanic.

"Well, hey yourself, Lani," he replied, rubbing the lump on his head. She came into the cockpit and settled on the floor, in a position to watch him work while he returned to what he was doing.

"You ever going to let me have a crack at flying this bird?" she asked, her gaze darting here and there along the control panel.

He flashed her a grin. "What do you want to fly this old antique for?"

She frowned at his insult. "I love this plane. Will you teach me to land in the water?"

He turned away, smiling. If he ever had a daughter, he'd love it if she turned out like this one.

"Why aren't you in school?" he said as he used a screwdriver to get a cable into place.

"I've got work study sixth period. I come here and work on mechanics and get credit for it."

"You like working on these smelly old machines?"

"I love it. I want to learn everything there is to know about planes. Then, when I have my own, I'll be able to work on it by myself."

He sat up and looked at her. She had a baseball cap on backward and grease on her nose. He liked that. "At the rate you're going, you'll probably have your own airline one of these days."

She grinned with the simple arrogance of innocent youth. "Why not?"

He shook his head, impressed with her. "What does your mom think about all this?"

"Oh, she hates it. She wants me to join the debate team like she did. I don't know, I guess she was some kind of student leader or something. But I'm not like that."

He turned to hide his grin. Student leader—that was a euphemism for what Sherry had been. But old stories like that about old friends were hardly appropriate for their children to hear.

Lani leaned forward, her face earnest and just slightly embarrassed. "Listen, is it true... I heard... Are you related to Jimmy Caine of Paukai?"

"Jimmy Caine?" He frowned. "No, I don't think..." And then it dawned on him. Little Jimbo, his sister's baby, indirectly the cause of his leaving Hawaii all those years ago. "Oh, sure," he corrected quickly. "Jimmy Caine's my nephew."

Lani's cheeks were suddenly pink. "Next time you see him, say hey from Lani Tanaka. Okay?"

"Sure." He frowned as he measured out a new length of cable and cut it. "You know Jimmy?"

She nodded, avoiding his eyes.

He glanced up. "Well, how do you know him? I thought kids out here had their own high school now. I thought they didn't go down to Paukai to school like they used to in my day."

"That's right." She squirmed and looked out the window. "But my cousin goes to Paukai High. I've seen Jimmy here and there."

He went on working, hardly thinking about what he was saying. "So you kind of like old Jimbo, huh?"

Her eyes widened and her face looked aghast. "Who said I liked him? I just said to say hey to him if you see him. That's all."

Mack carefully held back his grin. "What's he like?"

She looked at him curiously. "Haven't you seen him?"

"I haven't seen him since he was six months old."

"Oh, he's...he's..." Her eyes were bright with wonder and then she caught herself, pulling out a pair of dark glasses and shoving them on her nose to hide behind. "He's okay, I guess. Kind of tall, kind of thin...kind of cute." She grinned and suddenly she was a very pretty girl, making him do a double take.

He grinned back. "You're kind of stuck on him, aren't you? Come on, admit it."

She thrust out her chin. "So what?" She gave him a look, discarded the dark glasses and held out her hand for the cable, sliding into place to help him, needing no explanation of what he was doing.

"Have you got a boyfriend?" he asked idly as they worked.

She looked up in shock. "Me? No. I . . . I don't have time for dates and stuff like that."

"Uh-huh. But you like Jimmy."

She tilted her head to the side, considering. "He's different. He knows how to talk to a person about something besides the latest video or how drunk he was last weekend. And he doesn't make you feel like you should . . . I don't know, bat your eyelashes and wear tight dresses and stuff. He looks at you like a real person."

Jimmy was beginning to sound more and more like someone he was going to be pleased to meet. He only hoped the kid hadn't been cursed with the Caine legacy, like the rest of them. He screwed in the cable and tested it.

"Have you ever gone out with Jimmy?" he asked her.

"With Jimmy?" She was less candid now, more in control. "Oh, no. He's got a girlfriend."

"I see."

"Yeah. She's really pretty. She was Miss North Shore at the last Christmas pageant." She said it without envy, as though Jimmy lived on some other planet than the one she inhabited, and she liked everything about him, even his girlfriend.

He sat back and watched her work. She was good at what she was doing. It was a shame, really. This was one great girl, and if he remembered anything about high school, it was very likely that the boys mostly looked right through her. When he looked back, he had to admit to falling for looks and femininity himself. After all, who had he had a crush on all those years but Taylor, one of the prettiest girls in school. He didn't have much right to make moral judgments here. Still, it was a damn shame.

He looked off into the distance, toward the ocean, and he knew his sister was out there. He'd come to make peace with Shawnee, along with a few other things. And now he was beginning to get itchy about getting on with it. He needed to see her, see if they could patch up the past. And he wanted to see Jimmy. He moved restlessly, running a rough hand through his hair. This stuff with Taylor was getting complicated, much more complicated than he ever imagined it would. He was starting to care for her in a whole new way.

It had been comfortable having a crush on her all those years. He'd gotten used to it. But this was different. This was real, and what they had done this afternoon could have real consequences. He wasn't sure he was up to dealing with them. Real life wasn't a game.

"How's that?" Lani sat back and looked expectantly into his face.

He nodded. "Good work," he said simply. "I may have to hire you on to help me with some rewiring."

"Really?" She looked pleased as punch. "Cool."

"Cool," he repeated softly, a half smile on his face. But the smile faded as his mind went back to Taylor. The meeting with Bart Carlson had brought up some unpleasant realities he was going to have to deal with. And that wasn't cool at all.

As soon as Ryan came in from school he threw down his books and peered around the house. "Where's that guy?" he asked Taylor when he found her. "Where'd he go?"

Taylor put her hands on her hips and gave him a mock glare. "What happened to, 'Hi Mom, here's a kiss'?"

"Hi, Mom, here's a kiss," he repeated dutifully, puckering up and dropping a quick one on her cheek. "But where's that guy? He didn't leave, did he?"

"Mack is his name. And he's at the airport, looking after his plane."

"His plane?" Ryan's face shone. "He has a plane?"

She nodded. "I'm sure he'll take you to see it if you ask him." Then she frowned. She probably shouldn't encourage this. If Ryan got attached to Mack, his heart would just be broken when it came time for Mack to leave. She hadn't anticipated this sort of thing. One more problem to worry about. Speaking of which...

"Did anybody bother you at school?" she asked him anxiously, searching his eyes for the answer. "Did anybody say anything?"

Ryan frowned and looked at his shoes. "No. Why do you keep asking me that?"

She frowned, biting her lip. She was going to drive them all crazy, wasn't she? She had no right to put this struggle in Ryan's lap. Dropping to her knees, she put her arms around her little boy. "I'm sorry, honey," she said solemnly. "It's just that I want to make sure everything is all right with you. I'll stop asking if you promise you'll tell me on your own if anything bothers you. Okay?"

He hugged her. "Okay, Mom. Can I have a skateboard?"

She laughed and jumped up just as a horn honked in the driveway. "There's Mrs. Mueller to take you over to play with Teddy. I'll pick you up about five. Have a good time."

She waved as he hopped into the station wagon, then turned to the house, her mind a whirl of confusion. Just the day before everything had seemed so simple. Her only problem had been making Bart realize she was serious about fending him off and keeping her ranch. That was what Mack had been hired for. Now there was a new wrinkle. If she didn't watch out, she was going to fall much too hard for Mack. And that was very much against her rules.

This afternoon had been an aberration. No matter what, it couldn't happen again. She wasn't going to try to excuse what she'd done. But she wasn't going to repeat it, either. It had happened. It was over. That was that.

She heard Mack drive up. Anticipation fluttered in her chest and her heart began to beat a little faster.

"This is no good," she whispered to herself. "You've got to stop this." But she was holding her breath, listening for his footsteps, and she couldn't stop the rush of feeling as he came into the room. She forced herself to turn slowly. He was in the doorway, and when she saw his face, she knew this was not a time to smile in greeting.

He came into the room and stopped a few feet away from her, his eyes dark and somber. There was something there, something between bewilderment and anger. For a moment, he stared at her. She stared back, unable to imagine what on earth had happened, what had put him in this dark mood. When he finally spoke, his voice was low and rasping.

"Bart's in love with you, isn't he?" he said without preamble.

Her face registered her shock. "What?"

"I've just been talking to him." He frowned, watching her reaction. Of course it was true. Why hadn't he seen it before? He grasped the back of a handy chair, his knuckles white. "Come clean, Taylor. Why'd you tell me he wanted the land when really what he wants is you?"

Taylor stood with her hand over her mouth, her eyes wide with shock. She felt as though she'd been slapped. His accusation brought up a million conflicting emotions in her. And suddenly there was a lump in her throat, and she couldn't speak. Instead of answering, she turned away and walked toward the kitchen.

He followed her. She went to the sink and mechanically started rinsing dishes. She had to do something, anything, to keep back the tears that inexplicably wanted to fall. He stood right beside her. He was upset. She could feel his turmoil, but she couldn't do a thing to stop it. Not yet.

"Why didn't you tell me?" he repeated. "Has he asked you to marry him?"

Taylor closed her eyes and put down the dish. She had to stiffen her backbone and confront this. No crying. No avoiding reality. She'd been hiding from some of these truths herself. It was time to face the music.

Turning, she lifted her gaze to his. "Bart has hinted that he would like to marry me," she said evenly, her blue eyes holding his dark ones without wavering. "That's true. I told you he was always around after every incident, offering to protect me."

Mack slowly shook his head, studying her face, examining her eyes, the set of her jaw, the lines around her mouth, trying to find meaning where he could. "No, you didn't tell me quite that way. You told me he wanted to take over. You never told me his main objective was to get you."

There was a certain agony to this line of questioning. She knew she hadn't been completely open with him. But she hadn't thought it would be an issue at the time.

She held out her hands, palms up. "Don't you see? That's just a part of it all. Whatever he wants, he thinks he should have. And he wants things as a power base, not because he loves anything or anyone."

But Mack wasn't convinced, and his face showed it. There was a hardness in him now that she couldn't seem to penetrate. "I don't get it, Taylor. The man is crazy about you. He as much as told me so. How could a man like that do anything to hurt you?" He shook his head, his eyes full of doubt. "Are you sure he burned down the bunkhouse? Are you sure he did all those other things you told me about?"

She let her shoulders droop. She felt defeated all of a sudden. Now even Mack didn't believe her. "No, I'm not sure of anything. I told you that. Weren't you listening? I told you I suspected him, that's all."

"You supposedly suspected him strongly enough to hire me all the way from the mainland to help you fight him. That's pretty serious. It's a long way to go to get help holding off a man with a yen for you." Suddenly a light went off in his head. "Bart was the man kissing you, wasn't he?"

She frowned, shaking her head. "What man?"

"The one Ryan told me about. He warned me there was to be no kissing. He said there had been a man here kissing you, and he'd had to get tough to get rid of him. It was Bart, wasn't it?"

Taylor hesitated, then nodded. For a moment, she saw again the scene, with Ryan beating Bart with his small fists, shouting at him to leave his mother alone. Her heart filled with love for her little boy every time she thought of it. But how to explain all that to Mack?

Mack needed an explanation. He was sick over this. He felt lied to, used. He needed something from her, something to convince him, and so far he wasn't getting it. And at the same time, he wanted to rub Bart's face into the ground. In that moment, he hated Bart. His chest felt tight, and he rubbed the flat of his hand against his chin. He had to know it all.

"Did you ever date Bart Carlson?" he asked coldly.

She swallowed hard and nodded. "I . . . just twice."

"Oh, my God." He turned away.

She reached out and grabbed his arm, trying to make him understand. "I dated him twice and I knew it wasn't going to work. That's all. We were never . . . close."

He stared hard into her eyes, wishing he could believe her completely. "What did you hire me for?" he asked softly. "Is this some sick little game to make him jealous?"

The look on her face convinced him. She was horrified at the thought. "No! Oh, Mack, no, not at all. I don't like him. I didn't go out with him again because . . ." She stumbled, shaking her head, trying desperately to make him understand. "I could see he was going to start pressuring me toward sex and I couldn't bear the thought of sleeping with that man. Believe me, Mack."

He was relieved, but not satisfied. He wasn't sure why he felt it was his right to know all these things, but he did. It was as though he had to know. There was something driving him.

"You don't want to marry him."

"Oh, Mack. Of course not." She held his gaze with her own. "I told you when you first came how I felt about these things. I don't want to get married again. I didn't want to sleep with another man. As…as far as I'm concerned, Tom is still my husband. He always will be."

Mack flinched. Reaching out, he took her by the shoulders. "Taylor, that's just not right. Damn it, we both knew Tom. He was no paragon. I can't believe—"

She tried to twist out of his grip, her face contorted. "Don't! Don't you dare say another word."

But he wouldn't let her go. Holding her still, he forced her to meet his gaze. "Then why did you make love with me?" he demanded.

She stared at him dumbly. She couldn't answer that, not even to herself. Because she knew that right now, if he pulled her into the bedroom and locked the door, she would do it again. And that she couldn't explain to anyone.

"Why, Taylor? Tell me."

"I made love with you because I wanted to," she whispered, forcing the words out, knowing they contradicted all her rules, all her goals.

"Did it have anything to do with Tom?" he demanded, his eyes dark.

She thought for a moment, then shook her head, biting her lip.

His face relaxed a little and his left hand slipped up from her shoulder and cupped her cheek. "Of course it didn't have anything to do with him," he said gently, searching her gaze as though he thought he would find some secret he badly needed there. "Tom's dead, Taylor. He's gone." He pulled her closer, pressing her face to his chest, stroking her hair. "And you're alive. You're young. You still have a whole life to live. You can't bury yourself with Tom."

She closed her eyes. In the circle of his arms, she felt safer than she'd ever felt before. "But..." She tried one last time to remember her argument.

"Taylor, Taylor," he murmured, burying his face in her hair, his anger forgotten. "You are so beautiful, so alive, so full of life. You can be a mother and a widow and a lover, too. You have more to give than any other woman I've ever known."

She clung to him, letting his reassurance wash over her. But she knew she couldn't let this go on for long, or she would be lost again. She had to be strong.

"Taylor..." His mouth found hers, his lips nestling with hers, his tongue finding its way inside, and his hands began to move across her back.

Tearing herself away was the hardest thing she'd ever done. But she managed to do it, wrenching her body away from his warmth, feeling as though she'd ripped a part of herself away.

"Taylor, don't go."

She stared at him, wiping her mouth with the back of her hand. "Leave me alone, Mack," she whispered, her eyes tortured. "Don't touch me." There was a sob in her voice. "Please."

Whirling, she dashed away.

He stood where he was. His blood was running cold as ice. They were back to square one, with her saying, "Don't touch me." As far as he was concerned, that could only mean one thing. She regretted making love with him. Now that she'd had time to think it over, she realized it was a mistake.

He knew it was for the best. After all, she'd told him from the beginning that she was going to be true to Tom no matter what. He should have listened to her. He should have kept his hands off her.

Still, it was like a burning brand in his gut to face it. He couldn't have her. She wasn't his.

He slammed outside, looking for someplace to run to. Ordinarily when he felt this way, this torn with emotion, he would take his plane up or go to the range and shoot for a while. But he had to stay here. That was what he'd been hired to do. So he walked toward the cattle enclosure. The hired hands were there. It was time he got to know them.

Nine

Taylor lay very still and listened to the rain on the roof. It was two in the morning and she hadn't slept a wink yet. Her body was strung as tightly as a bow, and her mind was racing. She'd been over everything in her head, all the years with Tom, what she owed her son, how much she needed to hang on to the ranch. But she couldn't make it seem important the way she should, the way she usually could. It was all there. She acknowledged it. And still . . . And still . . .

Every time she closed her eyes, Mack's handsome face swam into view. She saw his body again, felt his hands on her skin. And then she writhed, tossing and turning, completely unable to find comfort. Wanting him was like a drum beating in her head, in her heart.

Slowly, like a woman possessed, she slipped out of bed and went to her door, listening in the hall, then padding to the door to Mack's room.

She didn't knock. Softly, she opened the door and went inside, closing it and turning the lock. Then she went to the edge of the bed and looked down.

He looked large and dark against the pale sheets. She lay her cool hand on his cheek.

"Mack?" she whispered.

At first he thought he was dreaming and he was afraid if he answered, or reached for her, he would wake up and it would all be over. She seemed to shimmer in the moonlight, her white gown transparent and yet silvery in the eerie glow.

She didn't speak again, but she saw that his eyes were open, and she reached for the tie at the neck of her gown, tugging on the ribbon, letting the garment fall to the floor with a long whispery sigh that signaled surrender.

He couldn't breathe. She stood before him, her breasts high and soft, the nipples flat and pink, like untouched flowers. Her arms were graceful as the limbs of a tree, her waist neatly curved in, her hips wide and generous, the dark area between her legs a mystery he knew he was about to be irresistibly drawn to. He looked into her face, at the hair that flew about her head like something made up in a fairy-tale world. She smiled, and he pulled back the covers, slowly revealing his body to her, his arousal, his desire.

She reached out and took him in her hands and he lay back, opening himself to her, laying himself bare to anything she wanted. And she wanted him all, every bit of his hard body and his tender love, and she explored him as though this was her first discovery, touching and caressing, making him gasp, making him turn and reach for her, loving her power to make him strong.

She came above him, letting him capture one nipple in his mouth while she took him between her legs, mounting him as though she had control, but then losing it as he came inside her, losing everything to the wild ecstasy of his body joining hers. He held back this time, letting her take the ride first, then turning her over and coming above her and taking her again, hardly letting her catch her breath before he let himself go and took her to his soul, searing himself and her with the same fire, melting them together in a heat that seemed to go beyond human endurance before it found its limit and died back, leaving them in each other's arms, both bodies wet with sweat.

Taylor closed her eyes and tried to think. She could hardly breathe. She felt as though she'd run ten miles and landed in a swimming pool full of honey. She was so tired, and yet she felt such sweet relief.

"You okay?" he muttered, shifting his weight off her but still holding her close. He wasn't sure what had happened. Toward the end his control had spun away from him and he'd reacted on instinct, all feeling, no sense.

"I'm okay," she whispered. "I'm more than okay." She wanted to tell him she was in heaven, that this had been the best experience she'd ever had, that he was a magician and his touch was magic. But she couldn't do that. She just couldn't do that.

He kissed her and she felt like purring, but instead, she drew back and looked into his face. "Tell me about your wife," she said.

His face registered shock. That was the last thing he wanted to talk about at a time like this. "Jill? You don't want to hear about her."

"Yes, I do. Mack, I have to know about her. Tell me."

He didn't want to think about Jill right now, much less talk about her. But as he looked into Taylor's blue eyes, he knew he was going to have to talk about it sometime. Why not get it over with?

Rolling over, he stared into the dark. "I met Jill in college, in California. She was cute and bouncy and I loved her from the first moment I saw her laying into a guy who'd come on to her at a party." Despite everything, he had to grin, remembering. "She could handle herself all right. We got married and moved to Florida. I went to work with the Drug Enforcement Agency. At first, she loved it, the excitement, the intrigue. But then a guy who worked with me was killed and she began to understand what we were up against. She started nagging me to quit."

Taylor shivered. "I don't much blame her."

He glanced at her and shook his head. "I couldn't quit. I was . . . almost obsessed with the job. I really felt like I was making a difference, helping to save the world from a great evil. You know what I mean?"

He looked at her hard, wondering if she saw the connection, if she saw how important it had been for him to prove to himself that he could do good, that he wasn't an outlaw at all. She was nodding, but did she really see it?

"Anyway, she hated it. I didn't realize how much until she left me."

Silently, Taylor put a hand on his cheek. He covered it with his, holding her to him.

"That shocked me, but I was angry, and it took another nine months and a few close calls for me to come to my senses and realize she was right." He took a deep breath. What came next was still hard for him to deal with. "I quit. And I went looking for her, hoping to get her back. But it was too late." Okay, here was the part that really hurt. "She'd married my old partner. And she was pregnant with his kid."

He waited, but the knife didn't pierce his chest as it usually did. The flash of black light didn't zap through his brain. The contraction didn't rip at the flesh between his shoulder blades. He took a deep breath and then another. Was it over? Was the pain really gone?

"So, that was that. I took off for California and bumped around different airports, doing free-lance work, until I saw your ad."

She slid next to him, warming his body with her own as though that would somehow heal him. "I'm glad you saw that ad," she whispered to him, and suddenly she realized she was telling the truth. If he hadn't seen it . . . if he hadn't ever come back into her life . . . She squeezed her eyes shut for a moment, not wanting to think about it. "I'm glad you came home, Mack."

He turned and took her in his arms, stroking her body with his large hands. He couldn't in all honesty say the same. Not yet. Because he wasn't at all sure if he really was home.

Mack leaned back and stretched drowsily against the cool sheets, just barely awake, still feeling the imprint of Taylor's body on his, still feeling the hot sense of her beside him, and suddenly he was aware that there was someone else in the room. He went stock-still. Only his eyes moved. There, at the side of his bed, he met the bright gray gaze of Ryan, watching him expectantly.

"Hi," the boy said.

"Hi," Mack answered, turning to his side and frowning. "What's up, kid?"

Ryan's gaze wavered as though he'd suddenly realized he shouldn't have come in without knocking.

"You were asleep," he said, as though that explained everything.

Mack nodded solemnly. "That I was."

Ryan hesitated, then pulled a piece of paper out from behind his back. "I brought you this," he said shyly, handing it to him. "I copied it from the 'cyclopedia."

Mack had to focus his eyes to make out what it was. At first it looked like a gray whale doing a clog dance. But then he began to make out details and realized Ryan had attempted a picture of a PBY. He turned to the child and saw the hunger in those young eyes, a hunger he immediately recognized. He'd lost his father at a young age, too. He knew how much a boy wanted a man to care about him.

"Hey, this is great," he said with a grin. "You want to go see my plane with me after school today?"

Ryan's eyes lit up. "Yeah," he said.

Mack nodded. "We'll go around four," he said. "We can stop somewhere for hamburgers, and I'll tell you stories about my great-grandfather. He was a pirate."

"Cool," Ryan said, eyes shining. Taylor's voice sang out, calling him, and he backed toward the door. "After school?" he repeated, just to be sure.

"After school," Mack agreed, and then Ryan was out the door.

Mack shook his head, laughing to himself. One moment he considered Morgan Caine a curse, the next he was using him to impress a little boy. For the first time in his life, he wanted to be a big man to a kid, and he was using something he'd always hated about himself to do it. Life was a funny deal all the way around. You had to take the good with the bad and use what you could, trying to keep some integrity while you were at it. He wasn't sure how he was doing on that score.

Levering himself out of bed, he took a quick shower and pulled on jeans and a polo shirt before venturing out to the breakfast table. Ryan was just finishing up and preparing to dash out the door to the car. When he saw Mack, he smiled shyly.

"Come on, Ryan," Taylor said impatiently, wasting barely a glance on the man she had spent most of the night with. "We're going to be late."

Mack grinned. "Hey, Ryan." He picked up his paper bag full of lunch and tossed it to him. "Knock 'em dead today, okay?"

Ryan's eyes were shining. "Okay."

Taylor caught the look on Ryan's face and her heart fell. "No," she whispered softly to herself. "No, Ryan, don't make a hero out of this man."

But she could see that it was probably already too late to stop that from happening. Glancing at Mack as he sat himself down at her table, she had mixed feelings. A part of her wanted to run into his arms, and another part wanted to banish him from the house. She had a hunch she knew which part was going to win this struggle.

She thought it over driving back from taking Ryan to school. She wasn't going to let herself get caught up in some torrid affair that would inevitably end up spilling ugliness into the rest of her life. She couldn't do that. She had to be firm.

She was friendly but cool to Mack when she got to the house. He took the hint and didn't push anything. But he sat back and watched her move through her kitchen and remembered what it was like to have that body in his complete control, and beads of sweat appeared on his brow. If she kept this up, it was going to be a long day.

But the day did pass routinely enough. He patrolled the ranch, riding Solomon without mishap, and she went in to town for supplies and to talk to potential customers. She was very busy, but underneath, she couldn't stop thinking about this incredibly dangerous man in her life.

She swore she was going to stay away from him. "It's okay," she told herself confidently. "You can give him up. After all, you gave up smoking. You gave up strawberry daiquiris. You gave up fats and sweets and lost fifteen pounds last year. You can give him up the same way."

She worked hard at it over the next few days. She tried being stern, keeping a frown on her face at all times and barking orders, wearing camp shirts and long, starched slacks and sitting like she had a ramrod up her back. She even started carrying a riding crop along with her wherever she went, smashing it against her leg as a reminder. "Pain, damn it," she would mutter to herself. "Pain, not pleasure."

But if didn't work. He'd play along for a while, and then he'd make some comment, or reach around and give her a quick kiss on the mouth, or make a joke that had her collapsing with the giggles, and it would be all over.

She tried staying away from the house. She spent hours out on the ranch, mending fences on her own. She'd tie tools to the saddle of Mint, her favorite horse, and ride out first thing in the morning. But after a day or two of that, Mack saddled Solomon on his own and came looking for her with a picnic basket and a bottle of wine. And they ended up making love in the tall grass beside the waterfall.

She tried inviting friends over a lot, including Sue and the Kimo Caine fan club. Sue had a wonderful time flirting with Mack, her violet eyes admiring his attributes even as she traded barbed banter with him. And the troika arrived loaded for bear, determined this time to get their man. Mack smiled and nodded and tried to be polite while they circled him and cooed.

"Do you remember?" they said over and over again.

And he nodded dutifully and pretended he did. That seemed to satisfy them. They each brought cameras and took turns leaning on him and having their pictures taken. And when they left, they had stars in their eyes. But the minute they were out of sight, his arms were around Taylor, and she was sliding her hands beneath his shirt and kissing his neck.

And then there were her good friends, Joyce and Larry. They were polite to Mack, but obviously worried about her. Just before they left, Larry pulled her aside and told her he had heard bad things about Mack and wanted her to please be careful. She had a hard time swallowing her resentment and keeping a smile on her face. She was being careful, careful as she could be. Couldn't they see that? Couldn't everyone?

But no matter how hard she tried to deny it, she knew one thing for sure. She'd fallen in love. It was impossible, it was irresponsible, it was against every tenet that she held dear. But no matter how much self-control she tried to use on the issue, nothing worked. She was in love. And most of the time, she was floating on air.

This love thing was very different from anything she'd ever experienced before. It hadn't been this way at all with Tom. They'd practically been children together and had grown up knowing they were meant for each other, as though it had been preordained by some all-knowing entity. They had just assumed that their lives would be spent making a life together. Their love had been very steady, and it had been very pleasant a lot of the time, hard sometimes, impossible a few times, but all in all, a good marriage.

But this feeling she had for Mack was very different. This had more highs and fewer lows. This was a trip to the moon, a ride down a waterfall slide on a hot day, a wild flight on a white Arabian across a desert sand. This was gasping and feeling her stomach drop away and feeling her heart beating so loud it almost deafened her. It was an excitement she'd never known before. And she was very much afraid that, once she lost it, she would never be the same again.

There were other people trying to help her put him out of her mind. Sue was one of them.

"Taylor," she whispered confidentially when she could get her friend alone. "I've got messages from Bart. I've got to talk to you."

"No. I don't want to hear anything from Bart."

"You've got to listen. Don't you know how he feels about you?"

Taylor shook her head. She wanted nothing to do with him.

Sue couldn't understand how she could be so obstinate. "Can't you see that if you married Bart, everything would be okay again? You could keep your ranch, you wouldn't have to worry about money ever again, your son would have a father to look up to. You would be set."

Taylor made a face. "Is that why you married your husband, Sue? Because he offered you such a good deal on a stress-free life?"

"Jason? Of course not. I was crazy in love with him."

Taylor laughed. "Yeah. That's right."

"Well, were you crazy in love with Tom?"

Did she have to tell the truth? Sue was a good friend. "Not really," she said evasively. "It was different with Tom."

"Then are you crazy in love with..." Sue's face fell. "Oh, no. You are, aren't you?" She groaned. "Oh, Taylor, tell me it isn't true."

"I'm not telling you anything. Sue, you're a good friend of mine, but this is none of your business."

Over the past few days she had become less and less apt to think about grabbing her shotgun. Was it because she felt safer with him here? Or was she just getting less paranoid?

When he wasn't with her, he was with Ryan. Ryan was in heaven having this handy playmate around at all times. It was, "Mack, will you take me sailing...swimming...in the airplane—" It didn't matter what, there was always something. And Mack would grin and Ryan would put his small hand into Mack's huge one, looking up at him with adoration, and Taylor would have to turn away, her heart breaking. She knew she shouldn't let this happen, let Ryan like Mack so much. And yet how could she deny her son this time? He needed a man's example so badly.

But Mack wasn't going to stay. They both knew that. Didn't they?

Ten

―――――

"**R**un away with me," Mack was whispering against her neck. "We'll fly to Tahiti, Australia, Bali, anywhere you want to go."

"Mmm." She closed her eyes and let her head fall back and savored his touch as he pushed aside the neck of her blouse so that he could get to her shoulder. He'd brought her to the airfield to see his PBY, and she was quickly learning to love it almost as much as he did. The pilot's chair was certainly comfortable, and as for the pilot . . .

"We'll dive for our dinner inside the reef and swim with tiny purple fish." His tongue outlined the ridge of her collarbone and she sighed with contentment. "We'll sit on the silver sand and sip Singapore slings as we watch the sun sink into the sea," he murmured in a masterpiece of alliteration that made her giggle.

"And we'll make love," she whispered, tracing the features of his face with her finger, "beneath a tropic moon as the gentle trade winds cover us with orchids."

He grinned. "You got it. Wanna go?"

She laughed, opening to his kiss, digging her hands into his hair to pull him tighter to her, luxuriating in his taste, his touch, his smell.

"Well, well, isn't this a tender scene?"

They sprang apart and turned to see Bart Carlson scaling the ladder and coming aboard. Taylor straightened, pulling her disheveled clothes together again, but feeling more annoyance than embarrassment.

"What do you want, Carlson?" Mack demanded, his face dark.

But Bart was looking at Taylor, frowning as though he was genuinely concerned. "Why are you always attracted to the wrong type of man, darling? First Tom, now Caine. What do you find to talk about with men like this?"

Taylor sat up straighter and glared at him. "It's none of your business, Bart."

He shook his head, putting on a sophisticated, world-weary look. "Ah, but it is my business, darling. I've had to pick up the pieces too many times for it to be anything else." He sighed, shaking his head again. "And I never get any appreciation for it, either. It's enough to make a fellow want to renounce good deeds and stop coming to the rescue."

Taylor took a deep breath in an effort to restrain herself. "You don't need to come to my rescue, Bart," she said evenly. "You never have and you never will. I can take care of myself."

His smile was oily. "We'll see about that, Taylor. We'll just see."

Mack took a step forward, looking menacing, feeling lethal. "I asked you what you wanted, Carlson," he said harshly. "State your business or get out of here."

Bart raised an eyebrow. "I came to try to talk some sense into you about selling this plane. But I can see that you are otherwise engaged at the moment." He sneered and turned as if to go, then looked back. "I guess you get her for now, Caine. But everyone knows you're a drifter. And I take consolation in the fact that I'll still be here after you're gone." His smile was eminently superior, and then he disappeared through the doorway and down the ladder.

Mack stared after him for a moment, then slumped down into a seat and stared at Taylor. "Nice guy," he commented.

She grimaced and rolled her eyes.

But Bart had said some things that raised questions. Mack frowned as he thought them over, then looked at her. "What was he talking about, Taylor? What did he mean about picking up the pieces?"

She glanced at him and then away. "Tom…we had some problems."

Reaching out, he caught her wrist in his strong hand. They'd reached a point where he felt he could push for answers. "What sort of problems?"

She hesitated. She didn't want to go into this. She'd vowed not to ever mention these things to anyone.

But Mack was special. She had to admit that. In some ways, he was her best friend now. As well as the man she loved.

"Tom…he had a few affairs." She looked out the window, wishing they could talk about going to Tahiti again instead of this. "It was no big deal. It didn't mean anything. I knew that. But Bart was a good friend to him in a lot of ways, and sometimes…he would go get him and bring him home."

He held her wrist and stared at where his fingers circled her small bones. He'd never liked Tom, and now he hated him. He only wished Tom was alive so he could kill him.

"It was funny," Taylor went on. "Tom always seemed to be able to go to Bart with his problems. From what I gather, the Taggerts always looked on the Carlsons as sort of the benevolent rich people next door."

"So Bart thought he could take over for Tom when Tom died."

"In a way. I guess." Turning to face him, she put on a smile that was only difficult to achieve at the very first. Once she got going, it was no problem. "Hey. Let's not talk about Bart. We were running away. Remember?"

He nodded slowly, but he couldn't get the mood back. He pulled her into his arms and held her tight, but for the moment, he couldn't fly.

The days went by and Mack felt as though he was moving in a haze and he wasn't sure if he wanted to come out of it. He'd made love with her once, twice, even three times with the certainty that he would soon have his fill of her, that this would assuage the yearning that had churned in him since his teenage years. All women were basically alike, weren't they? Taylor Taggert was no big deal.

But it hadn't worked out quite that way. He knew now that Taylor Taggert was a very big deal. Maybe too big a deal to handle. He felt like a man hanging on to a wild ride, not sure whether he should hang on while the rush lasted and risk smashing himself against reality, or let go and risk losing it all. Right now he was holding on for dear life. But he didn't know how long he could keep it up.

He spent his days working on the ranch, helping Taylor with what had to be done, getting to know the new cowhands, learning about cattle. He spent a lot of time with Josi, the old man who had been with the Taggert family since he was a kid. Josi told him tales of the old days.

"What exactly happened to the other cowboys?" Mack asked idly one afternoon. "I heard Bart Carlson ran them off or something."

"Ran them off?" Josi scratched his gray head. "Don't know 'bout that. All I know is the two of them got an itch to go to Honolulu and off they went." He shook his head. "I thought we would have a hard time replacing them. Miz Taggert was in a tizzy over it. But sure enough, the next day, these two new fellows we got now showed up, ready to work."

"You don't say," Mack mused, looking at where the men were working the herd. "Very interesting." His gaze sharpened. "I guess that was right around the same time the bunkhouse burned down, wasn't it? What happened there? Any ideas on who started the fire?"

Josi laughed, picking up a shovel and going to a stall to begin mucking it out. "Wasn't a who, mister. Was a what."

Mack frowned and followed him. "What do you mean?"

"Lightning. That's what did it. Saw it happen before. Weren't nobody home, luckily. The bunkhouse was empty. And we had one of those big lightning storms that only happen once every ten years. You know the kind? Place went up like a tinderbox."

Mack nodded slowly. It sure sounded logical. "Did you tell Taylor that you thought it was lightning?"

"Sure." He grinned. "But she got it in her head it was old Bart Carlson, and she won't listen to reason on that one. He showed up as soon as the fire trucks did. That man must have spies everywhere." He shook his head, more in admiration than anger. "She really gave it to him, and him trying to quiet her and hug her, like, and her yelling and telling him to keep off her property." Josi laughed. "I told her the man just wants a little love, and she told me she'd rather give him the sharp end of a pitchfork." He slapped his knee. "She's a feisty one. I don't think Bart's going to make any headway there." He flashed an impudent look at Mack. "Besides, seems like she's got interests in a new direction these days," he muttered, watching to see if his words were going to spark a negative reaction.

But Mack hardly noticed. He was mulling over the things Josi had told him.

"Hey, what about the stampedes? Taylor said there had been some."

"Oh, sure. A few weeks ago we were having them all the time."

"What caused them, do you think?"

Josi shrugged. "New cowboys. Didn't know what the heck they were doing. They've settled down now. We haven't had any trouble."

None of this seemed to jibe with the things Taylor had been telling him from the beginning. He mulled over the things Josi had said for a day or so before he brought it up to Taylor.

"Josi thinks it was lightning that burned down the bunkhouse," he said quietly one evening as they were sitting over coffee in the kitchen.

Taylor shook her head indulgently. "Josi also thinks that Pele, the goddess of fire, comes down out of Kilauea crater and sets house fires personally when she gets mad at people."

Mack looked at his coffee cup. "Are you saying I shouldn't trust Josi?"

"You can listen to Josi's stories. Just don't take them to heart." She looked at him curiously, suddenly realizing that he was doubting the things she'd told him. A part of her went cold. "Mack, what is this all about?"

"I'm just trying to get this straight, Taylor. I want to know exactly what Bart wants."

She stared at him. "You don't think he burned down the bunkhouse."

He shrugged, leaning back in his chair. "I don't know what I think."

"Mack, Bart was here in minutes, comforting me, telling me someone was out to get me, but if I would just live with him, he'd take care of me and everything would be okay. Do you honestly think I couldn't see right through him?"

He looked at her, hard. "Do you really think he did it?"

"Of course. I know for a fact that he paid the airfare for those hands to go to Honolulu."

He'd suspected as much. "Did it occur to you that it might be Bart who sent these new guys over?" he asked her.

Her eyes widened. "No. Do you really think so?"

He shrugged. "I don't know. But I think it's time I went over and had a long talk with Bart myself."

Her stomach dropped. That was exactly what she didn't want.

"I...do you really think that's a good idea? Bart is likely to say almost anything if he thinks he can get a rise out of you."

"I know that." Rising, he leaned down to kiss her softly on the mouth, then smooth her hair, watching as it fell about her shoulders in golden curls. "But we're not getting anywhere just sitting back and waiting to see what he's going to do next. I think I should talk to him. At least we might find out a bit more definitely where we stand."

He turned to go, and she bit her lip. She wanted to stop him and she wasn't sure why. Going to her desk, she pulled out her accounts and sat working with them, but actually she was just jotting down figures and not thinking about what she was doing. Her mind was on Mack and on what would happen when he went to see Bart. She didn't want him to go. Something told her that his going would change everything. And she wasn't ready to lose him yet.

* * *

Bart's house was stunning, a palatial mansion that could have been plunked down on a Southern plantation before the Civil War and looked right at home. His airstrip and hangars were off to the right, set off with bright lights. At any other time, Mack would have headed straight down to his collection and spent a happy evening looking the antiques over. But this was not a friendly visit. A butler opened the door, and a maid could be seen scuttling down the hall. Mack walked right in, refusing to let it intimidate him. He knew Bart was rich. So what?

He found him sitting in his library, nursing a snifter of brandy and staring into the garden. He raised one eyebrow as Mack walked in.

"Well, hello, Caine," he said without rising. "What do you want?"

Mack stood in front of him, legs set apart, hands easily at his sides. "I don't like playing games, Bart," he said evenly. "Let's get everything out on the table and see what we can do to resolve this situation."

Bart smiled, his eyes gleaming. "Did you come to make a deal?"

Mack frowned. "What are you talking about?"

Bart's eyes changed. "I don't know." He shrugged and looked innocent. "You came with the offer."

A quiver of tension shot through Mack's jaw. This had to be one of the most annoying men he'd ever met. "I don't have an offer. I just want to clear the air."

"If you didn't come to sell me your airplane, what did you come for?"

"To get a few things straight."

Bart sighed as though it was all just too, too boring. "Oh, all right. Get yourself a drink over there on the buffet, why don't you, and take a seat."

"I don't need a drink," Mack replied, but he sank into a chair opposite the one Bart was occupying. "I want to know what you're after, Carlson. What exactly do you want from Taylor?"

Bart looked suddenly woebegone. "A little love would be nice," he said sadly. "Barring that, plain old sex would do."

Mack lunged to his feet with both hands clenched into fists, but Bart laughed and waved for him to sit again.

"It was just a joke. Don't let's fight over it. I'd hate to have you arrested again."

Mack kept to his feet and glared at the man. "Your jokes aren't funny. Get to the point. Are you trying to pressure Taylor for her ranch? Or was all this just your charming way of courting her?"

Bart sobered and looked at Mack, his eyes narrowed. "She thinks I want the ranch, does she?"

"I think she's made that clear. She hired me to help protect her ranch from you."

"Is that right?" Bart threw back his head and laughed.

"What's so funny?" Mack demanded, stifling an overwhelming urge to put his hands around that scrawny neck and choke the life out of the man. His face was dark with anger.

Bart took a sip of his drink to settle himself. "Excuse me for laughing here, Mack. But there's something you don't know." He shook his head, smiling. "I probably shouldn't do this. But I'm going to let you in on a little secret. You see . . . Taylor doesn't own that ranch. For all intents and purposes, I do."

Mack stared at him for a long moment, then sank slowly into the chair.

Bart grinned. "So you see, all I'd need to do if I really wanted to get her off the land is to get the sheriff out there with an eviction notice."

Mack took a deep breath. He'd been expecting something bad, but this he hadn't foreseen. "You'd better explain," he said quietly.

Bart shrugged. "It's simple, really. Tom gambled. He gambled big. And he lost a lot of money, got in deep with some rather dangerous moneylenders. I bailed him out a few times, and finally he signed over a note on his ranch."

Mack felt sick inside. "And you took it."

"Hell, yes, I took it. I had to do something. I couldn't just keep throwing money down a rat hole."

Mack frowned, shaking his head. He'd known about Tom's gambling years ago, but he hadn't realized it had become a disease with him. The more he knew about Tom, the more he wished he'd stayed in Hawaii and made sure Taylor didn't marry him. But there was no point in going on about that now. It was much too late.

Still, some of the details didn't mesh. He frowned, shaking his head. "But then why would Taylor think... How could she not know about it?"

"He made me swear never to tell her. Everything is done through lawyers and accountants in Honolulu. She never sees the paperwork." He cocked his head to the side, considering. "But she's been getting pretty wily lately. She's turning into a real businesswoman. It's only a matter of time before she realizes how the land lies."

Mack felt a desperate wave of despair. What was this going to do to Taylor? She had so much of herself invested in the place, so much of Ryan's future depending on it.

"Why haven't you told her before this?" he asked, curious. Bart didn't strike him as the sort of man who held back bad news because of compassion.

But Bart looked surprised that he would ask such a question. "I'm a gentleman, Caine. Despite what you may think. Tom didn't want her to know." He sighed, taking another sip. "And there would be no reason for her to know, if she would only let me take care of her. It's what Tom would have wanted.''

It was Mack's turn to sneer. ''Yeah, but Tom's dead, Bart. What he wants doesn't matter anymore. It's what Taylor wants that counts.''

He nodded philosophically. ''And Taylor wants you. Yes, I've finally accepted that. For what it's worth.''

That was a relief. But it didn't help much. Mack shook his head. ''I still don't understand why Taylor thought you wanted her off the ranch.''

''She misunderstood.'' He smiled as though he'd thought of a little joke only he would understand. ''I may have presented my case badly from time to time, and she got the wrong impression. I tend to do things like that. It's just my way.''

The urge to maim the man, at the very least, was running strong, but Mack held it back. ''You did replace her workers, though. Didn't you?''

''Sure. I wanted to keep a closer eye on her.''

''Spies.''

He shrugged and grinned. ''It's the age of information, Caine. Get with it.''

''Did you burn down her bunkhouse? Stampede her cattle?''

''Never. You know I wouldn't hurt her for the world.''

''How about trying to cut her out with suppliers and customers?''

''That wasn't me. She's got competition, you know. She just hasn't adjusted to the cutthroat world as yet.''

''So all you wanted from the beginning,'' Mack said slowly, in a state of wonder, ''was for Taylor to be your girl.''

''Bingo. Give the man a blue ribbon.''

Mack shook his head ruefully. "You shouldn't have gotten quite so rough. If you hadn't started to push, she would never have contacted me to come help her."

Bart looked disgruntled. "I don't know what you mean by rough. I just put on the pressure here and there." He leaned forward in his chair. "You have to understand. I've been a friend of the family for years. I was probably the best friend Tom ever had. Like I said the other day, I was always the one who picked up the pieces."

"The affairs," Mack said softly.

"She told you about that?" He shook his head, frowning. "Poor thing. She went through hell with Tom sometimes. But she never complained." He sighed, swirling the liquid in his glass. "You knew Tom, didn't you? You knew he had a weak spot here and there. He was such a winner at everything in high school, he couldn't stand it when it turned out he couldn't be a star in college, too, and then in real life, he wasn't even a runner-up. That hit him hard. And whenever he got depressed, he picked himself up a bimbo and a bottle and took a room in a motel. It didn't mean a thing. He really loved Taylor. But he knew he wasn't good enough for her, and it ruined him. I used to go drag him back and clean him up and take him home."

Mack stood up. The room was closing in on him. He had to get out. Besides, he had a feeling Bart would go on all night if he gave him half a chance.

"So... are you going to tell her?" Bart asked, his eyes gleaming in the dim light. "I suppose you might as well. It's time she knew the truth. I'm only glad you're the one who's going to have to tell her."

Mack started for the door.

"Oh, Caine," Bart called out. "About that airplane of yours..."

Mack didn't say goodbye. He went to the airfield and sat in his plane in the dark for two or three hours before he went to Taylor's place. The house was quiet. Everyone was asleep. Silently, he slipped into Taylor's room. She stirred and welcomed him drowsily. They made slow, sweet love and she fell asleep in his arms. But he didn't sleep at all.

He watched the moon come and go, and then the purple splash across the sky. Taylor finally woke with the coming of the sun. She kissed his arm, then his shoulder, then his neck, but she didn't speak. And neither did he.

He'd thought about it all night and he still didn't know how he was going to tell her about Tom. She was working so hard to build the man's memory into something admirable. This was going to kill that. "Sorry, Taylor, your husband was a cheat and a gambler who gave away your land to pay off his gambling debts. Just thought you ought to know."

How was he going to soften the blow? What could he do? He looked down at her, his heart full of something he'd never felt before. He wanted to hold her so close and so tight that nothing would ever hurt her again. But that was impossible. Reaching out, he stroked her cheek with his index finger.

She lay very still, wondering what had happened with Bart the night before. She wasn't going to ask. Deep down, she didn't really want to know. She only hoped it wouldn't do anything to what they had between them. She knew this wasn't forever—but she was hoping for longer than this. She took his hand and kissed the palm, and then she smiled at him, and he smiled back.

Laying against the pillows, he stared at the ceiling. Her face was pressed to his chest, right over his heartbeat. Despite all the tangles he'd been wrestling with through the night, a sense of peace coursed through him. This was the way it could be. If he had a wife like Taylor...if he had a son like Ryan.... There was an ache growing inside him, a longing for exactly that. For a family.

He needed that, and yet he knew it wasn't going to be his. Not yet. Not here. This was Tom's place. He didn't belong here.

Still, he had another family. There was Shawnee. He had to patch things up with her. He'd been covering up the emptiness for years, but now he couldn't deny it any longer. There was a hole in his life, a piece of the puzzle missing.

"I'm going to have to get over and see my sister," he murmured, hardly realizing he'd said it aloud.

She raised her head and looked at him in surprise. "You mean you haven't contacted Shawnee yet? Why can't you just run over and say hi?"

"It's been seventeen years. I think I'll have to prepare more than hi."

"But she's your sister."

"She's also the reason I left."

"Oh."

He didn't like her tone. Turning, he looked her in the face, his eyes cool. "You didn't know that, did you? You thought I left because... What?" He wouldn't let her look away. "What was the scuttlebutt at the time?"

She tried to turn aside, but he caught hold of her. "Tell me, Taylor. What were they saying? That I skipped out to avoid doing right by Amy Fosselburg and her imaginary baby?"

Giving up, she stared right into his hostile eyes. If he wanted to get this out in the open, then maybe it was for the best. "That was part of it. And they said you left to avoid going to jail."

She saw something in his eyes, but she couldn't tell if what she'd said had hurt him or if it was something else. When he met her eyes again, he almost smiled.

"Do you want to know the real reason I left?" he asked softly.

She touched his face. "Of course," she said earnestly. "Tell me."

He looked past her, at the window where the morning light was just beginning to flood the green landscape with gold.

"Well, those stories were all wrong."

"Then what was it? What happened?"

His eyes narrowed, looking into a different time. "There is no denying I was wild in high school," he began slowly. "There were probably a lot of reasons for that. It didn't help that my father died when I was young and my mother left me and Shawnee with relatives a lot when we were teenagers, while she went off to look for work in Honolulu. Shawnee did her best, but she was only two years older and I didn't mind her very well. And then—I know it sounds crazy, but all the stories I grew up hearing from my relatives about Morgan Caine, my pirate great-grandfather, made it seem almost as though I was obliged to follow in the family footsteps and be an outlaw. I messed up. But it wasn't until senior year that everything went completely bonkers."

She nodded. She remembered it well.

"First I was kicked off the football team, a punishment I knew I deserved. I was a smart aleck and the coach didn't take my guff. I don't blame him. But all of a sudden, anything that happened, I got blamed. I had the rep. I got the blame. You know the time that alligator got left in the girls' bathroom? They said I did it, and I got suspended, but I swear, it wasn't me. I never touch reptiles. They don't like me."

She laughed and stroked his hair. The alligator had become the school mascot. She'd had to feed it once.

"The worst was when Bart accused me of robbing his house. It was true that a bunch of guys I sometimes hung out with did it. But I wasn't with them that night. I was doing a favor for someone—someone who could have cleared me right away if he'd wanted to." He shifted uncomfortably, glancing at Taylor and then away. "But he didn't, and I had to spend a night in a cell."

Taylor wrinkled her nose. "Who was it?" she demanded.

He shook his head, avoiding her eyes. "It doesn't matter now. The point is, everyone was ready to believe I did it. There are probably a lot of people who still believe it."

"Mack..."

He put a finger to her lips. "Don't say it," he told her softly. "Just let me get this out." He touched her hair, taking a curl and winding it around his finger. "I was so frustrated, so angry that no one trusted me. But I knew I could always count on my sister. Shawnee was there for me every time. But then... I don't know if this really happened or if I was just getting paranoid. But it seemed as though she was beginning to doubt me, too. I went kind of nuts. I quit school and started practically living out at the airfield. I didn't want to see anyone or anything that wasn't connected to flying. Shawnee tried to get me to go back to school, tried to get me to think about college, and I didn't treat her very well. In the meantime, she had a baby. The father was some tourist who took off right after he got her pregnant. We all hated his guts for that. Well, Shawnee took the baby over to Kona to visit my aunts and she asked me to look after my little brothers, Kam and Mitchell, while she was gone. I gave her a hard time, but I did it. Right after she left, though, who should show up but the tourist, coming back for another fun-filled summer in paradise." He shook his head, his mouth twisted.

"I wanted to beat him to a bloody pulp, but I held off. I told him Shawnee was gone, had married someone else and never wanted to see him again. He left, and I was pretty proud of myself. I'd gotten rid of the scum. So when Shawnee got back a few days later, I told her about it, thinking she would be grateful. Imagine my surprise. It turned out she was still in love with the jerk. She started yelling at me about a baby's right to know his father and all this garbage.'' He stopped and took a deep breath. "And then she got into what a failure I was, how I couldn't even do this right, how she'd given up on me and wanted me out of her life. She said I was ruining the family, that she wanted me gone before it rubbed off on my brothers. So I split. I sold my car and bought a ticket to L.A., and that's the end.''

Taylor could close her eyes and imagine his pain, imagine how he'd felt hearing the person he loved most in the world, the person he practically considered his mother, saying things like that. It was no wonder he'd worked so hard to prove he wasn't a bad guy after all. Now if only she could get him to relax and believe it himself.

"I'm sorry that happened to you, Mack," she told him softly, stroking his arm. "It was rough. But you did okay on your own. You went to college and carved out a career for yourself. Maybe—"

"Don't say it was for the best," he warned her. "Just don't say that."

Okay. She wouldn't say that. But could she say this? "I think you turned out pretty well," she said tentatively.

He looked at her and a slow grin started. "For a high school dropout?" he said mockingly.

She shook her head. "For a bright, strong, talented man who had some obstacles to overcome. I think you're pretty special."

He kissed her softly. "I think you're the best," he whispered.

She touched his cheek. "But I still think you should go and see your sister. You have to go see her right away," she told him solemnly. "You have to see..."

"See if she still thinks I'm scum?" He tried to smile, but it wasn't easy. "Yeah, you're right. I've got to bite the bullet." His eyes clouded. "I never realized it was going to be so hard to do," he muttered softly, mostly to himself.

"Go see her this morning," Taylor said. "Then come back and we'll go into town for dinner for a change. Okay?"

He didn't answer. He wasn't going to go see Shawnee yet. He had other things to wrap up first.

Taylor slipped out of bed and began to dress, and he watched her. He should tell her now. He should get it over with. She was going to find out about Bart holding the note on her ranch soon enough. He'd better prepare her for it. And to be prepared, she would have to know about Tom's gambling.

Damn Tom. How could he have done this to a woman who was so good to him? She was working so hard to preserve his memory for her kid, and to preserve his legacy, too. This was going to kill her.

"Taylor," he began. "You know that stuff you were telling me about Tom yesterday . . . ?"

She whirled, bright spots of color in her cheeks. "No, Mack," she said firmly. "No, please. I shouldn't have told you. I . . . I can't say things about Tom, not to anyone. He's Ryan's father. It is so important for Ryan to have a good image of him."

He stared at her, thinking of Jill, thinking of all the other women he'd ever known. Would any one of them have done something like this for him? Not likely. Taylor was a very exceptional person. She deserved some exceptional treatment herself.

She deserved anything a man could do to make her life better. And there was damn well something he could do. And maybe it was time to do it.

Sliding out of bed, he grabbed her and kissed her hard, then released her and turned away.

"I'm not going to have time for breakfast," he told her brusquely. "I've got somewhere I've got to be."

Eleven

The first thing he did was to go to the airfield and borrow Bob Albright's phone to call Honolulu. He'd seen the name of Taylor's law firm when she was working on some papers, and he got in touch with her lawyer quickly enough. It took a little longer to convince the man that he had any right to talk to him about Taylor's case, but once he'd explained what he wanted to do, he got cooperation. And some good advice.

Next stop, Bart Carlson's.

Bart was eating a late breakfast on his terrace when Mack came charging in.

"Okay, this time I'm ready to deal," Mack said without preamble, flopping down on a chair at Bart's wrought-iron table.

"How delightful to see you," Bart said calmly, putting down his newspaper. "Would you care for a poached egg?"

Mack made a face. "I want to get this settled. I've called the law firm of Whitmore, Chang and Hattori in Honolulu. They've assured me they can have the paperwork ready by this afternoon, and they'll fax it over."

Bart's face looked more alert than Mack had ever seen it. He slowly put down his fork and folded his napkin. "Go on," he said softly.

"Here's what I want you to do," Mack said. "I want you to tear up that note you have on Taylor's place. I want you to agree to leave her alone. And I want you to promise you won't tell her about Tom's gambling."

Bart blinked like a snake in the sun. "And what exactly is going to be my incentive to do all these things?" he asked.

Mack reached into his pocket and took out something that jangled. He looked at it for a moment, then held it out for Bart to see. "The keys to my PBY," he said firmly. "Agree to my terms. It's the only way you'll get her."

Bart started to laugh. He laughed softly at first, but then he got louder, until finally his laughter was echoing down the hill and over his huge lawns. He laughed and laughed, but at the same time, he reached for the keys.

Taylor knew something was up. She just didn't know what it was. She ran to the window at every little sound, hoping it was Mack coming back. But he didn't return until after noon, and by then, she was a nervous wreck.

"Mack!" she cried, flying into his arms. "Where have you been?"

He kissed her long and hard and then he held her against his chest, stroking her hair and savoring the feel of her so close. He closed his eyes. It felt like praying. She was the best thing that had ever happened to him. And now he was going to have to leave her.

"I've been too busy, Taylor. Bottom line, I've got to go see my sister now."

"Of course." She raised her head and looked into his eyes, and suddenly she was afraid. "We . . . we talked about that earlier."

He released her and turned toward his bedroom. She followed, a hollow feeling growing inside. Stopping in the doorway, she watched as he pulled out his duffel bag and began throwing clothes inside.

"What are you doing?" she asked, her voice so hoarse she barely recognized it.

"I'm going, Taylor. Bob Albright is giving me a ride to Paukai."

"No!"

He turned and looked at her pale face and something twisted deep inside. He wanted to drop the bag and take her in his arms and promise never to leave. But he knew he couldn't do that. That wouldn't work in the long run. It was time to go.

"I had a long talk with Bart. He's agreed to leave you alone. You won't hear from him again unless you need him and you initiate the contact."

She was staring at him, hardly hearing his words. What did she care about Bart? Mack was leaving. She wasn't sure she could stand it.

"I wish you would stay," she whispered, her eyes huge smudges in her ashen face.

He couldn't look at her. "I have to go. It's time. And you're going to be okay."

She cleared her throat, holding back tears she was determined not to shed in front of him. "I won't be okay without you," she said softly.

It broke his heart. He pulled the bag closed with a fierce yank that almost broke the rope. He sat for a moment and stared at the bag. There was a strange stinging in his eyes, and he had to wait a moment until he had control of it.

"You'll be okay," he said again. "You're strong, Taylor. If you survived losing Tom, you're certainly not going to be devastated when I go."

She blinked, not sure what on earth he was talking about. "Why do you always want to compare yourself to Tom?" she said in bewilderment.

Finally he looked up and met her eyes. Standing, he swung the bag over his shoulder. "Because back when you had a choice, Taylor, you chose Tom."

His words were a splash of cold water and she stood in shock as he left, striding through her house and out the front door. She couldn't move. He was right. What could she say? He was right.

Bob dropped Mack off in front of the Paukai Café. Someone in his family had been running the place for at least the last fifty years, and from what he'd heard, Shawnee was pretty much the one in charge these days.

The place looked pretty good, sort of chic and touristy, but that was better than run-down and dirty. He walked in and dropped his bag on the floor. A young man of sixteen or so came to greet him.

"Table or counter?" he asked cheerfully.

Mack stared at him, at his tall, handsome good looks, at his familiar-looking green eyes, and he grinned. "You're Jimmy, aren't you?" he said.

The boy nodded, then looked more sharply at Mack. "You look like...are you a Caine, too?"

Mack nodded. "They used to call me Kimo around here."

Jimmy's face broke into a smile that lit up the room. "I thought so. You look a lot like my uncle Mitchell. Hey, wait until Mom sees you."

But Shawnee had already seen him. She was coming across the room, pushing past the customers, looking hardly a day older than she'd looked seventeen years before. Mack

looked at her, feeling suddenly shy, suddenly scared, like a
kid again, a kid who had done something wrong and wasn't
sure how he was going to be received by the ones he loved.
Her green eyes looked him up and down, her hand over her
mouth. And suddenly those eyes were swimming with tears
and her arms were open wide. She remembered him. There
was no hesitation from her at all. And then he was in her
embrace, and they were both crying, holding tight and sob-
bing, and a love too deep for words was creating a bond that
would never be broken again.

Taylor sat and stared at the columns of figures she was
trying to add up. They didn't make any sense at all. She
couldn't even remember what she'd written them for.
Throwing down her pen in disgust, she jumped up and
paced the floor again, just as she always did these days.

"You've got to get used to this," she lectured herself
fiercely. "Quit being such a crybaby. He's gone, and that's
all there is to it. Life goes on."

Life should be going on. Life had been just fine before
Mack came along and messed everything up. Oh, there had
been a problem or two with Bart, but otherwise . . .

The problem with Bart seemed to be solved. She hadn't
heard a thing from him in the week Mack had been gone.
How Mack had fixed that, she didn't know.

One whole week. And she was still alive and kicking.
There had been times those first few days when she hadn't
been too sure she would make it. She couldn't sleep. She
couldn't eat. She looked at her arms. They were skinnier
than ever. But she was surviving.

Not that it was a barrel of laughs around here. Every
night, Ryan started in on the questions again. Why had
Mack left? Where had he gone? Why had he gone? When
was he coming back? She was going crazy trying to figure
out answers for him.

That was it. She was going crazy. She was going nuts. Mack had taken over her mind.

No. He'd taken over her heart. And for some reason, she couldn't let go.

His last words echoed through her head by the hour. "When you had a choice, you chose Tom."

"But wait," she wanted to say. "That wasn't a real choice. I didn't really know you."

But she knew deep in her heart that that was no excuse. She'd chosen Tom because he was the safe one. It had been the easy thing to do. And Mack had been much too scary. She'd chosen Tom because she hadn't had the guts to go for what she really wanted.

Was that all that was holding her back now? Guts?

No, it was more than that. What Bart had said about Mack was partially true. In some ways, he was a drifter. No one would have expected him to stay here and work this ranch with her. He was a flyer. He would want to go where the flying jobs were. She had been right to let him go. It would never have worked.

Then why was she crying every hour on the hour? Why did she find it impossible to put on makeup and get dressed and go to town, to act like a normal human being?

"Because you're in love, you ninny," she scolded herself mercilessly. "You're in love and you don't have the guts to go with it."

There was a sound in the driveway and she raced to the door, her heart in her throat. Could it be...?

No. It wasn't.

Lani Tanaka brought her rattletrap motorbike to a stop and waved.

Taylor waited in the doorway, trying to hide her disappointment. "Hi, Lani. Come on in." She had to work at being cordial. It was hard, and she hated Lani for not being Mack.

"Hi." Lani was carrying a brown paper bag. She came in and looked around, flipping her dark glasses to the top of her head. "I've been meaning to come by all week and bring you this stuff. Mack asked me to give it to you. He had it left over after he cleaned out his plane the other day." She handed over the bag and Taylor opened it, spilling out a rag she'd loaned Mack, and her scarf, which she must have left on the plane the other night when he'd given her the grand tour. "I just haven't had time 'cause we've been having finals at school and . . ."

Taylor stared at the items. "Why was he cleaning it out?" she asked woodenly.

"He was getting it ready to move over to Bart's airstrip."

"To Bart's?" Taylor looked at Lani in amazement. "What are you talking about? Why would he move it to Bart's?"

"Don't you know? He sold it to Bart. Which really shocked me. I mean, he always said it was like his firstborn child and he would never, ever—"

Taylor sank into a chair, her face sheet white. "No, that can't be."

"I know. Weird, huh? But that's what he did."

"I can't believe it."

"From what I heard, Bart made him an offer he couldn't refuse."

"Oh, my God." Taylor sat staring into space. A whole new way of looking at things had suddenly opened before her. She was almost blinded by the light.

Lani shuffled her feet and shrugged, then turned toward the door. "Well, I guess I'll see you later, Mrs. Taggert."

Taylor barely lifted her hand to wave. "Thanks," she murmured vaguely, staring straight ahead.

In a few minutes, the sound of Lani's little putt-putt motor could be heard disappearing down the lane. But Taylor didn't seem to hear it.

"Oh, my God," she whispered again, still staring. "Mack. Oh, my God."

Slowly, she reached for the telephone. She had a few calls to make. She had a few things to do. But did she have the guts? Did she?

Twelve

Two hours later, she interrupted Bart at his pool table, practicing his shots.

"Why, Taylor, darling," he said, genuine pleasure shining in his eyes. "It's so good to see you."

She nodded but didn't smile. "You give Mack his plane back, Bart," she said firmly. "Give it back, and I'll give you the Taggert ranch for good."

He opened his mouth, then closed it again. Turning, he carefully put away his cue then faced her again.

"I don't want the ranch," he said simply. "I want that PBY."

Her mouth quirked with impatience, her eyes cold and humorless. "You've had the plane for one whole week and that's enough," she said, frowning.

He shook his head, half laughing, not sure what to make of her. "You're insane."

"No. I'm not." Her blue eyes narrowed. "I'm mad, though. You've taken advantage of me and mine for the last time. I want Mack to get his plane back and you to have the ranch. I know all about the note you held. I know how Mack got you to tear it up." Her eyes blazed. "As an interested party, I should have been consulted before all this was done. Now I'm putting in my two cents' worth. We're going to do it my way."

He searched her eyes. "How did you find out? Did Mack tell you?"

She snorted. "Hardly. I found out about the note when I called my lawyer and demanded to know what was going on. Didn't you think he might tell me?" She shook her head in disgust. "I suppose Tom made over the note to you to cover gambling debts."

Bart looked shocked. "You knew about that?"

"Of course I knew. I was the man's wife, Bart. I knew him very well."

Bart hesitated. "Where's Caine?" he asked suspiciously.

"Mack is gone. He has nothing to do with this. But I want him to get his plane back."

He studied her face and his eyes clouded. He shook his head. "He's not worth it, Taylor. Don't you see that? He's a drifter. He'll never marry you."

"There's one more proviso," she went on as though she hadn't heard. "You've always had a soft spot for Ryan. And the way things are going, it doesn't look like you'll be having a son of your own. So I want you to lease the Taggert ranch to Ryan when he turns twenty-one and leave it to him in your will."

He gaped at her. "Be serious."

"I am serious. I've never been more serious in my life."

He laughed shortly. "This is preposterous. I don't know why I'm even listening to this."

She stood firm. "Bart, you're always talking about how you were the best friend Tom ever had. We both know he was the best friend you ever had, too. He did plenty for you. I know about the money-laundering deal two years ago. And the way he covered for you with the trade commission. All in all, I'd say you owe me."

Bart blinked. "Pure speculation, my dear," he murmured.

"Oh, no, it's not. And I'll use it against you if I have to."

Something flashed in his evil eyes. "Say that in court, Taylor. Tell it to a judge and see what happens."

He stared at her hard, and she stared back. He wasn't going to budge. She could see that.

"Okay," she said with a weary sigh. "You're not going to cooperate. I'll have to go to the last resort." She tossed back her hair and glared at him. "I'm going to cut off your water."

For the first time, pure panic sparked in his gaze. "What?"

"I'm going to cut off your water. I'll divert the river and make sure you don't get a drop. That land of yours is awfully dry on that side. You won't be able to graze a billy goat there once I turn you off."

His knuckles were white. "You can't do that! I need the land on that side. You know the EPA is doing a study of all my property on the west side because of that endangered mouse or something. I can't graze that side until they're finished. You can't take away my water. It never rains there behind the mountain...."

"I know, Bart. That's the whole point. I'm hardballing you, just like you always do to everyone else. Take my offer or lose your water."

Bart was silent for a long moment, and then he shook his head, his eyes sparkling with as much admiration as resent-

ment. "Taylor, Taylor, we could have made such a beautiful pair, you and I."

"Too late." She turned and looked at him. "My lawyer
will be here by one with the papers. Get your signing hand
limbered up. There will be plenty of places for your signa-
ture."

She didn't wait to see if he was going to laugh or cry.
When you came right down to it, she didn't much care.

The ride out to Paukai went in a flash because her mind
was racing and she felt as though she was on fast-forward
the whole time. If the truth be known, as furiously as she
was thinking, she hadn't thought anything through. She was
going on pure instinct and emotion. "And it's about time,
too," she muttered as she drove.

She stopped in front of the little café and took a deep
breath before going inside. She wasn't sure what she was
going to say. She only knew she had to find Mack. She had
the guts. She was finally sure of herself there. Now she had
to find out if she was going to get any of the glory, after all.

The place was almost empty. The lunch rush was over.
She stood uncertainly in the doorway, blinking in the dim
light, suddenly terrified. What if he didn't want her? What
if he turned her away? She looked around the room and
didn't see anyone who remotely resembled him. What if he
wasn't here at all?

A lovely young woman in a pink *holomuu* with her long
brown hair in a braid down her back, came gliding up.

"Hi," she said, holding out her hand. "You're Taylor
Taggert, aren't you?" She smiled as Taylor nodded and
shook hands. "I had a feeling you might show up. I'm
Shawnee, Mack's sister. He's told me a little about you."
She laughed. "Not that he's exactly been a chatterbox. You
know Mack. But he said enough to make me think we would
be seeing more of you."

Taylor looked anxiously around the mostly empty room. "Where is he? I've got to talk to him."

"Come on over and sit down. Let's get to know each other a little first."

She didn't want to talk. She wanted to find Mack. But she reluctantly followed Shawnee, admiring the long, fitted Hawaiian dress the girl wore so well, and sat down at a little table decorated with an orchid sitting in a glass vase.

Shawnee smiled at her warmly. "It's been so good having Mack home. We've spent hours and hours talking about the old days, and all the relatives have been trooping by to see him. All these years, I've had no idea what became of him."

"Do you mean to tell me he never so much as sent a Christmas card in all those years to let you know he was okay?" Taylor asked, horrified.

Shawnee nodded. "That's the thing about some men, Taylor. They have this ability to take off and not look back."

Her gaze went into the past for a moment, and Taylor realized she was thinking about the father of her son.

"But, anyway, he's come back. And he's promised to keep in touch from now on." Shawnee smiled. "And I understand, if it hadn't been for you, he probably wouldn't have come back to Hawaii." Reaching out, she squeezed Taylor's hand. "Thank you so much. For years I've wanted to tell him how sorry I was for the way he left before. You can't know how guilty I've felt. I was supposed to be the one nurturing and raising him, and look what I did."

Her eyes were still haunted by the past. Taylor's heart went out to her.

"You were too young for that much responsibility," she reminded her.

Shawnee smiled quickly. "Yes, in a way, I was. But with our father dead and mother always gone, and our aunts living on the other side of the island, there wasn't much choice." Her eyes dimmed, suddenly blurring with a hint of tears. "He got blamed for a lot of things back in those days that weren't his fault. I knew that, and still, I just made it worse."

"He's told me something about it."

Shawnee nodded. "The worst, of course, was Bart Carlson having him arrested when he wasn't anywhere near that man's house."

Taylor nodded. "He told me he was helping someone else that night." She hesitated, but she had to know. "Was it Tom Taggert, Shawnee? Please tell me the truth."

Shawnee nodded. She understood feelings. "You see, what happened was, Tom had gone down to Hilo and done some gambling with some low-life types he should have stayed away from. He ended up losing his mother's ruby ring to them."

Taylor gasped. She had that ruby ring in her jewelry box right now.

"He was desperate to get it back before his mother found out. So he came to Mack for help. Mack had a reputation for knowing how to deal with people like that." Shawnee shrugged. "They certainly weren't friends, but I've never known Mack to turn anyone down. He went down to Hilo with him. I don't know how he did it, but he got the ring back for Tom." Shawnee shook her head. "And then the next day, when Mack was accused of breaking into Bart Carlson's house, Tom refused to back up his alibi. I have to admit, that made me mad."

Taylor sighed. "Of course it did." But she believed it. Even back then, when Tom had been the golden boy of the high school, he'd had a streak of behavior he'd tried to hide from her. She'd known he sometimes went to Hilo and did things he would never tell her about. Later on she'd realized better what some of those things had been. She had known Tom about as well as anyone could, and she knew what he was capable of. He had his good points, but sometimes his bad side seemed to outweigh them.

"Anyway, I didn't mean to get off on that long story. I just want you to know that Mack thinks a lot of you."

Taylor's smile was tremulous. "I think a lot of him, too."

Shawnee grinned. "I can tell."

Taylor smiled back. "What...what did he say about me?"

Shawnee sobered. "He said he thought you were still too caught up in the past to fall in love with him."

Taylor sat back, horrified. "That's wrong."

Shawnee stared at her for a moment, then reached out and took her hand again. "I thought so," she said softly. "I wish you luck. I hope you find him."

Taylor smiled, then frowned as the full meaning of her words sank in. "What do you mean?"

Shawnee shrugged. "He's gone. He left this morning."

Taylor's heart sank. "Left! Where did he go?"

She shook her head. "I don't know. He wasn't sure himself. He said he'd call later in the week."

Taylor jumped up from her seat. A new urgency was pulsing through her. "I've got to find him. Do you suppose he went to Honolulu?"

Shawnee rose, too. "That stands to reason. But, Taylor..." She caught her by the arm and held her for a moment, looking earnestly into her eyes. "You know he's a flyer. He's going to roam. I don't think it's possible for him to stay in one place too long, even your ranch, even if he wants to."

Taylor's smile was beneficent. Shawnee didn't know the ranch was a moot point. "I know that." She gave Mack's sister a quick hug. "Thank you for everything. I'll let you know if I find him."

She dashed out the door and into her car, stopping at the bank to draw out a large amount and put it into traveler's checks. Then she raced home.

"Ryan!" she cried as she ran into the house. "Are you home yet?"

He'd just arrived. His schoolbooks were still in his backpack and on his back.

"Pack your bags, honey." She threw her arms around her child. "We're going on a trip."

"A trip?" He was definitely interested. "Where?"

She laughed, dancing a little jig with her son. "We're going hunting. Man hunting. And whom do you think we're going to be hunting for?"

"Mack!" He danced, too, then remembered his masculine code of small boy behavior and stopped short. "Where is he?"

"I don't know, Ryan. But we're going to look for him very hard. And if we're lucky..."

"We'll find him!" Ryan cried. "Can I pack my video games?"

They rushed into the little terminal at the airfield. It was closer than driving all the way down to Hilo. Her biggest fear was that Mack would fly out of Honolulu before they could get there. Loaded down with bags, they made their way to the counter.

"I need a plane, quick," Taylor said to the gray-haired man, who looked up in surprise. "Can I charter something that will take me to Honolulu? I've got to get there as quickly as possible."

Bob blinked at her and at her short son and he had to smile. "Well, I've got a Twin Apache all gassed up and ready to go. The pilot's in her, too, looking her over. He'll fly you out. You can leave right away."

It seemed like a miracle. Taylor's shoulders sagged with relief. "Oh, thank you. Thank you. How much—"

"Just give the money to the pilot once you get there." He grinned and waved as they hurried away. "Aloha," he called after them. "Have a good trip."

Taylor led Ryan across the service area, heading for the plane, and anxiety began to catch up with her again. She had no idea where they were going or what they were going to do once they got there. She was hoping to find Mack at Honolulu International Airport, but she had no guarantee that he would be there. He could be in Kona, visiting relatives, or on Waikiki, soaking up the sun. She had no way of knowing. But she couldn't stay home and not give this a try. She had to find him.

"Wait." Ryan stopped at the bottom of the steps that would lead them into the Apache. He looked at his bundles in dismay. "Oh, no, I left my blue bag at the terminal."

"Well, run on back and get it," Taylor told him. "I'll go on into the plane and talk to the pilot. Hurry!"

He dropped his bags and took off while she turned and climbed aboard. She could make out the outline of the pilot. He was sitting in the cockpit, checking out the controls.

"Hi," she called out. "Bob Albright said you would be able to fly me and my son out of here this afternoon. I hope that's all right."

Mack sat very still. He could hear the voice. He knew it sounded like Taylor. But he didn't want to turn around and find that his mind was playing tricks on him.

He could hear her stowing away her luggage. He was going to have to turn around and find out if it really was her any minute now. But he stretched it out, savoring the anticipation.

"Hello?" she called again. "Is it okay?"

He turned in his seat and looked at her. It was Taylor. His heart began to thud in his chest.

She was squinting in the gloom and it was obvious she couldn't really make him out. Rising slowly, he leaned through the entryway and grinned at her.

"It's fine with me, lady," he said softly. "Just tell me where you want to go."

She swayed, emotion filling her with such elation she could hardly breathe. It was Mack. She'd already found him.

His eyes were deep and dark and filled with something she couldn't name, but it was good, and she began to shiver, holding her arms around herself, laughing softly as she looked at him.

"Where do I want to go?" she repeated, loving him, hoping with all her heart that he might love her back. "Tahiti. Australia. Maybe Bali."

His wide mouth twisted and he stepped closer. "I see. Any particular reason for those destinations?"

She nodded. "I'm chasing down a dream," she said, her voice trembling. "Mack. I'm taking you up on your offer."

He reached forward and she reached out and their hands met. He laced his fingers with hers. "What offer?" he asked.

She blinked at him. Surely he hadn't forgotten. Laughter shone in her eyes. "You said we could run away together."

He laughed softly. "You're kidding, aren't you? How could you leave?"

She smiled, secretly wondering what he was going to say when he realized he had his plane back and that she was no longer tied to the ranch. She was free. She and Ryan were ready to go with him anywhere he wanted to go.

If he really wanted them to. Her smile faded. After all, it was easy to say he wanted her to run away with him when he knew it was impossible. Now that it was an actual possibility, maybe he would think twice.

And he was thinking twice. And three times, and four. And all that filled his head was the certainty that he had to tell her that he loved her. He tried. But somehow his tongue just couldn't form the words. The only other woman he'd ever said them to had been Jill, and look what had happened there.

But that wasn't going to happen here. No. It couldn't. Taylor wasn't like Jill.

Still, he stared at her with all his emotions in his eyes and he couldn't say it.

"I went to see your sister," she told him.

That surprised him. "You did?"

"Yes. We talked about you, about what a bum rap you've had all these years."

His fingers tightened on hers. "Do you really believe that?" he asked.

She nodded. "Mack," she said, sincerity shining in her eyes. "I believe it with all my heart. I know you now. I know what kind of man you are. You're probably the best man I've ever known."

There was no relief, no surge of joy, just a warm sense of peace because for the first time, he believed she really meant it. "Thank you," he said softly. "Taylor... I missed you."

Joy leapt in her veins. "I missed you so much," she murmured. "I thought I was going to die without you."

He pulled her close and kissed her, touching her hair, her face. "You wouldn't have been without me. I was going to stay right here. That's why I asked Bob for a job here at the airfield. I wanted to be where I could help you if you needed it. After all, that's what you hired me for."

"Really?" She drew back and stared at him. "You would really do that for me?"

He nodded slowly. "Don't you get it, Taylor?" he said, his voice husky with emotion. "I...I love you."

There. He'd said it.

She stared at him, stunned by his words. "Oh, Mack," she whispered, touching his face. Tears were beginning to pool in her eyes.

"I've loved you since high school," he admitted gruffly. "Only I didn't really know it until now."

The tears were coursing down her cheeks, and there was something choking her throat. She couldn't speak. Instead, she clung to him, pressing her face to his chest, and sobbed as though her heart would burst with happiness.

"Taylor." He stroked her hair, but all this crying worried him. "Taylor, are you okay? Did I say something wrong?"

"No." She shook her head, half laughing, half crying. "Oh Mack, I love you, too. I just can't believe this is happening."

Finally the sense of relief was flowing through him. There did seem to be a light at the end of this tunnel after all. But there was one more thing.

"Taylor, about Tom..."

"Mack, we don't have to talk about Tom. I know all about everything, his gambling, the whole deal. I tried hard to pretend I could erase his past, but now I know how impossible that is. I definitely want Ryan to think well of his father, but the way I've been going about it, I realize now that I was trying to build up some idealistic image for him to worship." She reached up and kissed his lips very softly. "Right now I think it's more important for him to have a flesh and blood live man to learn from than a dead plaster hero."

Deep inside, he'd known she would come to her senses about this. "There's one more thing, Taylor," he said,

smiling at her. "And it's important to me. I have to know.
Do you want more children?"

"You mean your babies?"

He nodded, searching her eyes.

"But Mack, wouldn't that tie you down?"

He gave her an incredulous look. "Why does everyone
think I'm so anxious to head off into the sunset? I've done
that, Taylor. I've been gone for seventeen years. And now,
all I can think about is how much I want a home and a
family... and you."

"In that case..." She grinned. This was almost too much
happiness for one person at one time. "I would love to have
your babies."

He laughed. "They'd be your babies, too," he reminded
her. "And I guess we'd better get the formalities out of the
way." He dropped to one knee in front of her. "Taylor
Reynolds Taggert, will you marry me?" he asked, love
shimmering in his eyes.

"Oh, Mack," she said happily. "I will."

Rising, he took her in his arms and kissed her hard and
long, until a little hand interrupted, tugging on his jacket.

"Hey," Ryan said. "We found you."

They looked down at him and laughed.

"Does this mean we gotta stay here?" Ryan asked, disappointed. "I want to go to Honolulu." He looked at Mack
brightly. "Could we still go? Could you be our pilot?"

Mack cocked an eyebrow. "I don't know, kid. How much
do you pay?"

Ryan looked surprised but willing. "I got some money in
the bank. Maybe Mom would write a check."

Mack hid his grin and shook his head in mock denial.
"Gotta be cash, kid. I only deal in cash."

Ryan looked stricken. "I...I got money in my piggy bank
but I forgot to bring it," he said, his face puckered with
worry.

"Oh, Ryan!" They both reached out and brought him in for a group hug.

"Don't worry about it, kid," Mack told him with open affection. "We'll go to Honolulu. We'll go out to dinner and take you to the dolphin show and everything. Okay? Because we've got something to celebrate."

"We do?" Ryan looked from one to the other of them brightly, as though he understood it all without having it explained. "Great." But when you came right down to it, he could do without the sappy stuff. He made a face and pulled away and ran forward to the cockpit. "I'll be copilot. Okay?"

They laughed again. "No silly love songs for him," Taylor said.

"Not yet," Mack agreed. "But just wait. When he's older..." He took her in his arms, kissing her with tenderness, holding her with love. "He'll find out how good a love song can be."

She sighed, happier than she'd ever been before. "I feel like I'm in a dream," she murmured.

His arms tightened around her. "No more chasing after dreams, Taylor," he whispered against her lips. "Reality is much, much sweeter."

*   *   *   *   *

Don't Miss THE DADDY DUE DATE *Next Month*
From Silhouette Desire

It's our 1000th
Silhouette Romance
and we're celebrating!

Join us for a special collection of love stories by the authors you've
loved for years, and new favorites you've just discovered.

**It's a celebration just for you,
with wonderful books by
Diana Palmer, Suzanne Carey,
Tracy Sinclair, Marie Ferrarella,
Debbie Macomber, Laurie Paige,
Annette Broadrick, Elizabeth August
and MORE!**

Silhouette Romance...vibrant, fun and emotionally rich! Take another
look at us!

As part of the celebration, readers can receive a FREE gift AND enter
our exciting sweepstakes to win a grand prize of $1000! Look for
more details in all March Silhouette series titles.

**You'll fall in love all over again
with Silhouette Romance!**

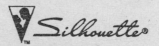

**Relive the romance...
Harlequin and Silhouette
are proud to present**

 ™

A program of collections of three complete novels by the most requested authors with the most requested themes. Be sure to look for one volume each month with three complete novels by top name authors.

In January: **WESTERN LOVING**   Susan Fox
                                  JoAnn Ross
                                  Barbara Kaye

Loving a cowboy is easy—taming him isn't!

In February: **LOVER, COME BACK!**   Diana Palmer
                                     Lisa Jackson
                                     Patricia Gardner Evans

It was over so long ago—yet now they're calling, "Lover, Come Back!"

In March: **TEMPERATURE RISING**   JoAnn Ross
                                   Tess Gerritsen
                                   Jacqueline Diamond

Falling in love—just what the doctor ordered!

Available at your favorite retail outlet.

REQ-G3

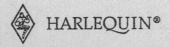 HARLEQUIN®

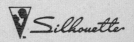 *Silhouette*

SILHOUETTE® *Desire*®

SAXON BROTHERS

**An exciting new trilogy from
JACKIE MERRITT**

**Chance, Rush and Cash—three sinfully sexy brothers who
would turn any woman's head! Don't miss:**

March **WRANGLER'S LADY**—Chance is one handsome
Montana rancher, and this *Man of the Month* knows what
he wants—and how to get her!

April **MYSTERY LADY**—The desert heat of Nevada is
nothing compared to the sparks that sexy Rush ignites in
one mysterious woman!

May **PERSISTENT LADY**—The untamed wilderness
cf Oregon and one persistent female are no match for
determined bachelor Cash!

**Let the SAXON BROTHERS keep you
warm at night—only from
Silhouette Desire!**

SDSAX1

 **SILHOUETTE® Desire®**

 **SOMETHING Wild**

by Ann Major

Take a walk on the wild side with Ann Major's sizzling
stories featuring Honey, Midnight…and Innocence!

IN SEPTEMBER, YOU EXPERIENCED…

WILD HONEY Man of the Month
A clash of wills set the stage for an electrifying romance for
J. K. Cameron and Honey Wyatt.

IN NOVEMBER YOU ENJOYED…

WILD MIDNIGHT
Heat Up Your Winter
A bittersweet reunion turned into a once-in-a-lifetime adventure for
Lacy Douglas and Johnny Midnight.

AND IN FEBRUARY 1994, LOOK FOR…

WILD INNOCENCE Man of the Month
One man's return sets off a startling chain of events for
Innocence Lescuer and Raven Wyatt.

Let your wilder side take over with this exciting series—only from
Silhouette Desire!

SILHOUETTE... Where Passion Lives

Don't miss these Silhouette favorites by some of our most distinguished authors! And now you can receive a discount by ordering two or more titles!

SD	#05772	FOUND FATHER by Justine Davis	$2.89 ☐
SD	#05783	DEVIL OR ANGEL by Audra Adams	$2.89 ☐
SD	#05786	QUICKSAND by Jennifer Greene	$2.89 ☐
SD	#05796	CAMERON by Beverly Barton	$2.99 ☐
IM	#07481	FIREBRAND by Paula Detmer Riggs	$3.39 ☐
IM	#07502	CLOUD MAN by Barbara Faith	$3.50 ☐
IM	#07505	HELL ON WHEELS by Naomi Horton	$3.50 ☐
IM	#07512	SWEET ANNIE'S PASS by Marilyn Pappano	$3.50 ☐
SE	#09791	THE CAT THAT LIVED ON PARK AVENUE by Tracy Sinclair	$3.39 ☐
SE	#09793	FULL OF GRACE by Ginna Ferris	$3.39 ☐
SE	#09822	WHEN SOMEBODY WANTS by Trisha Alexander	$3.50 ☐
SE	#09841	ON HER OWN by Pat Warren	$3.50 ☐
SR	#08866	PALACE CITY PRINCE by Arlene James	$2.69 ☐
SR	#08916	UNCLE DADDY by Kasey Michaels	$2.69 ☐
SR	#08948	MORE THAN YOU KNOW by Phyllis Halldorson	$2.75 ☐
SR	#08954	HERO IN DISGUISE by Stella Bagwell	$2.75 ☐
SS	#27006	NIGHT MIST by Helen R. Myers	$3.50 ☐
SS	#27010	IMMINENT THUNDER by Rachel Lee	$3.50 ☐
SS	#27015	FOOTSTEPS IN THE NIGHT by Lee Karr	$3.50 ☐
SS	#27020	DREAM A DEADLY DREAM by Allie Harrison	$3.50 ☐

(limited quantities available on certain titles)

AMOUNT	$	
DEDUCT: **10% DISCOUNT FOR 2+ BOOKS**	$	
POSTAGE & HANDLING	$_____	
($1.00 for one book, 50¢ for each additional)		
APPLICABLE TAXES*	$_____	
TOTAL PAYABLE	$_____	
(check or money order—please do not send cash)		

To order, complete this form and send it, along with a check or money order for the total above, payable to Silhouette Books, to: **In the U.S.:** 3010 Walden Avenue, P.O. Box 9077, Buffalo, NY 14269-9077; **In Canada:** P.O. Box 636, Fort Erie, Ontario, L2A 5X3.

Name: _____

Address: _____ City: _____

State/Prov.: _____ Zip/Postal Code: _____

*New York residents remit applicable sales taxes.
Canadian residents remit applicable GST and provincial taxes.   SBACK-JM

Silhouette®